D1039616

I HAVE THREE PROBLEMS.

Dan Welch told the Vice President of a big Hollywood studio that I have an idea for a movie. Or a whole series of movies. She wants to meet me.

PROBLEM 1: She's probably going to want to hear that idea.

PROBLEM 2: I don't live anywhere near Hollywood.

PROBLEM 3: I can't tell you now, but you'll find out, I promise.

I REPRESENT SEAN ROSEN

Jeff Baron

GREENWILLOW BOOKS

An Imprint of HarperCollins*Publishers*

This book is a work of fiction. References to real people, events, establishments, organizations, or locales are intended only to provide a sense of authenticity, and are used to advance the fictional narrative. All other characters, and all incidents and dialogue, are drawn from the author's imagination and are not to be construed as real.

I Represent Sean Rosen
Copyright © 2013 by Jeff Baron
First published in 2013 in hardcover;
first Greenwillow paperback edition, 2014

All rights reserved. No part of this book may be used or reproduced in any manner whatsoever without written permission except in the case of brief quotations embodied in critical articles and reviews. Printed in the United States of America. For information address HarperCollins Children's Books, a division of HarperCollins Publishers, 10 East 53rd Street, New York, NY 10022.
www.harpercollinschildrens.com

The text of this book is set in 12-point Bruce Old Style.
Book design by Paul Zakris

Library of Congress Cataloging-in-Publication Data
Baron, Jeff, (date).
I represent Sean Rosen / by Jeff Baron.
pages   cm
"Greenwillow Books"
Summary: With the help of his "manager," a thirteen-year-old boy
sells a movie idea to a major Hollywood studio.
ISBN 978-0-06-218747-5 (trade ed.) ISBN 978-0-06-218748-2
[1. Motion picture industry—Fiction. 2. Middle schools—Fiction.
3. Schools—Fiction. 4. Humorous stories.] I. Title.
PZ7.B26889Iam 2013
[Fic]—dc23   2012042076

14 15 16 17 18 CG/OPM 10 9 8 7 6 5 4 3 2 1
First Edition

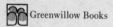

This book is dedicated to my various parents, relatives, and friends, who always encouraged me to be the kid I wanted to be.

have an incredible idea. Unfortunately, I can't

chapter 1

I have an incredible idea. Unfortunately, I can't tell you what it is. People have stolen my ideas before. They pretend it was their idea, and then they don't even ask me to be part of it. That's a mistake, because I understand the idea way better than they do, and if I'm not there to explain it, they usually get parts of it wrong. Then it doesn't really work. Or it sort of works, but it could have been a hundred times better. It's a waste of a good idea.

I'm not saying this happened fifty times. Maybe five. They never give me credit, which is fine because the way it turned out, I don't really want credit.

I'm not counting the little things, like I'm in class and I say an answer out loud and someone hears me and raises his hand and gets called on and it's the right answer.

They never thank me, either. I don't mean getting up and saying, "I'd like to thank the Academy, God, and most of all Sean Rosen, who in his own special way, made me look smart today." I'd settle for a quiet "Thanks, man," or even a little nod in my direction.

So I have this great idea. I can't tell you what it is, because even if you didn't mean to, you'd end up telling someone, because it's so cool. All I can tell you is that it has something to do with entertainment. In fact, I think it will change the way people think about entertainment.

Like for example, remember when people used to only watch TV shows on TV? Now we watch them on our computers, on our phones . . . anywhere we want. I'm telling you this to prove that the way people think about entertainment can actually change. I'm not saying that putting TV shows on phones was my idea. My idea is actually a little bigger than that.

I know the company I want to be in business with. I'm not going to tell you their name. You know them. They're huge. They're a huge company in the entertainment business. I looked them up online. Their offices are in California and New York. I live in between.

Since this is my first time trying to work with a big company, and since I know which company I want to be in business with, I think I should practice on another company. Just in case I do something wrong.

I learned this from one of my grandmothers. She likes to practice things before she does them. Like say she has a doctor's appointment tomorrow, with a doctor she never saw before, in a place she doesn't really know. Most people would just put the address into their GPS and follow the directions. Or if they didn't have a GPS (my grandmother doesn't), they'd go on MapQuest or Google and print out directions.

Grandma prints out the directions, but instead of just using them to drive to the doctor, first she uses them for what she calls a "trial run." She drives to the doctor the day before her appointment, just to be sure the directions are right. It makes my dad crazy (she's his mom). "You're not only wasting time, you're wasting gas." Grandma doesn't care. She likes to know what she's doing.

The website of the trial run company gives you their e-mail address, their telephone number, their regular street address in California, and their fax number.

We don't have a fax machine, but I can send faxes from my computer. I figured it out for my mom. Every time I send a fax for her she gives me two dollars, which is less than the copy place she used to go to. The last time she had to send a fax, I offered to teach her how to do it from her own computer. She said, "No thanks. Do you have change for a five?"

I decided not to send them a fax. If they only have one fax machine for the whole gigantic company, it's probably broken half the time. And if it's not, whoever gets them has to read like a thousand faxes every day. I don't trust that person to get my fax to the right person. I don't trust that person to not be in a bad mood and throw my fax in the garbage. If I had that job, I probably wouldn't do that, but I've never gotten a thousand faxes.

I'm sending them a letter. Like a letter on a piece of paper that you put in an envelope. Hardly anyone ever does that, so the person at the company who opens actual letters might be happy to have something to do.

This is my "trial run."

Dear _____ (the big entertainment company I'm not so interested in),

I have an idea that I'm pretty sure can make your company millions, if not billions of dollars. All I can tell you right now is that this is an idea relating to entertainment.

Please ask the person at your company who works on new ideas to call me. My number is 555-555-5555 (not my real number). Any time after 3 would be fine. Believe me, it's a really good idea.

Sincerely,
Sean Rosen

I took a piece of my dad's stationery. I'm not going to use it for the letter. My dad is a plumber. I'm not saying that a plumber would never have a good entertainment idea. I actually never heard of that happening, but it could. I took his stationery to get ideas for *my* stationery. If you're wondering why a plumber has stationery, it's for giving people bills.

I designed my stationery and I put my letter on it. It looks good. I already know how I like to do my signature. I practice a lot during history. I figured out how to print envelopes on our printer.

I rode my bike to the post office because I want to mail it right away. I don't want it to sit in some metal box all day waiting for a truck to come and drive it to the post office. I also want to pick out the right stamp.

I think the Love stamp might be confusing. There's a nice Oklahoma stamp, but I'm not from Oklahoma. I got the Thomas Edison stamp. He also had some good new ideas.

The next few days were very, very long. Have you ever waited for a phone call? It might come in the next five minutes or it might never come at all. You keep checking your phone to make sure it's on. And when you have to turn it off, like in school, you keep turning it back on to see if they called while it was off. You want to stop thinking about it, but you can't. You get mad at whoever was supposed to call, and you get mad at yourself, because you're acting crazier and crazier.

I woke up in the middle of the night and realized that I told them to call me after 3, but I forgot to tell them that I don't live in the same time zone as them. Their 3 isn't the same as my 3. And I never said 3 PM. I just said after 3.

I got out of bed and wrote a second letter telling them that when they call me, it should be after 3 PM, *my* time. After reading it, I decided not to send it. I just kept my phone near me all the time. Most of the time I held it in my hand. I learned that if you ever have to hold the phone while you're charging it, like when you're sleeping, you don't get electrocuted.

I mailed my letter on a Monday, and when I got home from school on Thursday, there was an envelope from the entertainment company waiting for me. It was kind of thick.

I put my phone down (finally), and thought about where to open the envelope. Maybe this sounds conceited, but I'm thinking about the future. Like when I'm on a talk show, telling the story of where I was when I read the letter that started my career.

Which is funny, because this started out as a trial run. I don't know how it happened, but some time between mailing *my letter* and getting *their* letter, I actually got excited about being in business with my second-choice company.

It's like when you pretend to be sick so you can stay home from school, then you actually get sick. No it isn't. It's like when there's only one scoop of chocolate and one scoop of butter pecan left in your freezer. You want the chocolate, but your friend says he thinks he's allergic to nuts. You don't completely believe him, but you take the butter pecan, even though you never tasted it and never wanted to. Then you find out you love butter pecan.

I decided to open the letter in my old tree house. It's not actually mine, but I used to go there. And it's not really a house. Just a tree where my friend's dad nailed a big piece of wood. We're actually not friends anymore.

The idea was that once you climbed the tree, you'd have somewhere to sit that was more comfortable than a branch. The piece of wood is actually *less* comfortable than a branch, but if you bring a pillow or two, it's not too bad.

I took two pillows, and when I was up in the tree and comfortable, I opened the letter.

Jeff Baron

Dear Mr. Rosen,

Thank you for your interest in _____ (the entertainment company). In response to your letter, it is the official published policy of our company not to accept unsolicited submissions of any kind or nature.

For your information, no one outside the legal department of this company has seen your letter. No one at this company ever invited you to make a submission.

_____ is an extremely large, diversified corporation with thousands of active projects and properties throughout the world. We take no responsibility for any coincidental similarity between your work and ours.

All of our projects are protected by copyright, and despite the possibility that your material may be similar in some way, or even identical, to one of the properties we own, your unsolicited submission does not qualify you for any legal rights or compensation with regard to our property.

We can assure you that we defend and prosecute nuisance

lawsuits to the fullest extent of the law. Should you wish to approach this company again, we suggest that you do so through a talent agent or management firm.

If you can believe it, this letter went on for another three pages. I didn't know what they were talking about half the time, and they probably don't either. It's like when you download a new computer program. You start out reading the Terms of Agreement, but it just goes on and on. You want to use the program, so after about two paragraphs you give up and click "I Agree."

But who knows? Maybe near the bottom of the Terms of Agreement there's something that says, "Starting today, I agree to give you all the money I earn for the rest of my life, plus my dog." You agreed to it because you got bored reading all those big words.

By the way, I don't have a dog. I want a dog. At least I think I do. If you've never had something, you think you want it, but since you don't really know what it's like, maybe you don't actually want it. It doesn't matter anyway because my mom definitely doesn't want one. If you ask her why, the only thing she'll say is "I'm not a dog person." My dad isn't a cat person, so that's that.

Obviously, the legal department never even read my letter. THERE WAS NO SUBMISSION. I didn't tell them anything about my idea. I just asked them to give me a call. I slept with my phone all week for nothing.

And no matter what they said in their letter, I'm sure they don't have an idea that's similar or identical to my idea. I didn't tell anyone that I sent this letter, but if my grandmother knew, she would say, "This is why you do a trial run."

chapter 3

NO MORE FISH.

was fries-texting my mom. We were at the kitchen table having dinner. She and my dad were talking about some concert they went to twenty years ago, so she didn't see my plate with those words spelled out in fries. My mom thinks it's healthy to have fish once a week. Once a week is okay, but tonight was the second time. I wanted to eat my fries, so I cleared my throat and pointed. She said, "Cute. The fish was on sale. Sorry."

I decided not to tell my parents about writing to the entertainment company, or the obnoxious letter I got back, but I did ask them what a nuisance lawsuit is. They know. My mom's a nurse.

She told me that nurses have to have insurance, because people are always suing doctors and nurses and hospitals. "You made me get a CAT scan during the Super Bowl. I'm suing you for fifty million dollars." That was her example. I don't know if it really happened.

My dad has to have insurance too. I guess he had a nuisance lawsuit once. Someone said their water was too hot and they got burned, and it was my dad's fault. He started explaining to me how it wasn't his fault at all because the family did something to the water heater to make the water hotter than it's supposed to be. It only took a minute of hearing about the water heater before I told my dad, "I Agree."

The next day after school I got back to work. I'm still mad about that letter, but I can't think of anything I can do about it.

Since the company I want to be in business with probably has the same rules as the company I wrote to, I guess I should get a talent agent or a management firm.

I always thought I would have an agent. Once

in a while in school when someone, even a teacher, asks me to do something, just to be funny I say, "You'll have to talk to my agent." Not everyone thinks it's funny.

Different people laugh at different things. I notice it all the time at the movies. Sometimes I'm the only one laughing. I can't always explain why, but I just think something is funny. Even if no one else laughs, it doesn't mean I'm wrong. It's funny to me.

Sometimes I feel like I'm the only one *not* laughing. I hate that feeling. At first I think maybe I didn't get it. But I actually did get it. I just didn't think it was funny. Then I start wondering why everyone else thought it was. It's distracting.

I went online and did some research about agents. I've heard of some of the big agencies in the entertainment business, but I don't know anything about them. They have the world's smallest websites. They don't say the names of the agents. They don't say who they're the agents for. But I read that an actor I like works with a certain agency, so that's the one I picked.

I don't want to waste another week waiting for an answer, so this time I'm calling. Just about the only thing on this agency's website is their phone number.

For Hanukah last year my parents got me a really good digital voice recorder. I use it for my podcasts. And every once in a while I record something else. Like a phone call I want to remember.

OPERATOR: **SIA.** (a big famous talent agency—not their real initials)

ME: **Hi. Are you the agent for David Boone?** (a super funny actor—not his real name. Trust me, you know him)

OPERATOR: **I'll connect you with Steve Stevens.** (he must be David Boone's agent—not his real name either)

This was easy. They put me right through to a really big agent. Then a woman answered.

WOMAN:	Steve Stevens.
ME:	Oh. I was expecting you to be a man. That's interesting that your parents named you Steve.
WOMAN:	No. They named me Delilah.
ME:	Oh. I thought I was being connected to Steve Stevens.
WOMAN:	You are. I work for him.
ME:	Oh. Good. He's who I want to talk to.
WOMAN:	Who's calling?
ME:	Sean Rosen.
WOMAN:	Steve's in a meeting. Will he know what this is about?
ME:	I don't know. Is he psychic?
WOMAN:	I have no idea. Why?
ME:	If he was psychic he would know what this is about.

(she doesn't say anything)

You're right. It isn't that funny. Anyway, he's the

agent for David Boone, right?

WOMAN: Yes. Are you a producer?

ME: No. Well, yes. I do produce things.

Then no one said anything for about five seconds.

ME: How did you know I was a producer?

WOMAN: If you're calling about David Boone, you're either a director, which you're not, because I would have heard of you, or you're a producer.

ME: Oh. I'm not calling about working with David Boone. Though I plan to some day. No. I'm actually looking for an agent.

WOMAN: For what?

ME: For me.

WOMAN: What do you do?

ME: Oh. Well . . . it's a little
           hard to say exactly.

WOMAN: Well, what have you done?

ME: Oh, quite a few shows.

WOMAN: Which shows?

ME: Oh. I don't know if you've
           heard of them.

WOMAN: Try me. I know most of the
           TV shows.

ME: Oh. These weren't on TV.
           They were actually assemblies.

WOMAN: Wait a minute. How old are
           you?

ME: Thirteen.

WOMAN: Wait. Are you a little boy?

ME: No. I mean I'm a boy, but I
           wouldn't exactly say I'm
           little.

WOMAN: I thought I was speaking to
           a woman producer.

ME: Named Sean?

WOMAN: There are women named Sean.

ME: I'm not one of them.

WOMAN: Good-bye, Sean.

My voice recently started to change. A lot of people used to call our house and think I was my mom. It was annoying. When I was eleven I got my own phone, so it stopped. Now if you're calling me, you know who I am.

I know my voice is changing because of my podcasts. When you make podcasts and edit them yourself, you get to hear your voice a lot. I hated it at first, but I got used to it. If you listen to my newer podcasts, I sound older now and more like a guy. But maybe not to Delilah.

chapter 4

I know that some kids have agents. I was watching a talk show and I heard a kid actor say, "I was in my friend's backyard and I got a call from my agent telling me I got it." He was talking about a part in a TV show. How did he get that agent?

"Hell if I know." My dad was in the room watching TV with me. He didn't say it in a mean way. He just doesn't know. "Sorry, Seany. I wish I could help you with this stuff. I guess you got the wrong dad."

I wasn't actually asking my dad "How did he get that agent?" like I thought he would know. It was just one of those times you're thinking about something, and you say it to yourself out loud, but the person in the room with you thinks you're talking to them. It happens all the time. By the way, my dad is the only person who ever calls me "Seany."

"What do you need an agent for?" I wasn't sure I wanted to get into all this with my dad, so I didn't answer. He said, "I could be your agent." That's nice of my dad to volunteer, but I can't picture him talking to this huge entertainment company. He doesn't speak that language.

There actually is a special show-business language. I've been learning it. Last year, my parents asked me what I wanted for Christmas, and I said a subscription to *The Hollywood Reporter*. I've been reading it every week. *The Hollywood Reporter* is a magazine about show business, the business part of it. It talks about movies and TV and music and games, sometimes theater and books. When you subscribe, you get it online and also a paper copy. I like the paper copy because when you read it in public, people in show business know you're in show business too. Actually, that hasn't happened yet. There aren't many people in show business where we live.

You might be wondering why someone named Sean Rosen is getting Christmas presents. Actually, my dad is Jewish and my mom is Catholic, and we celebrate everything, more or less.

"Hey, Sean!" It's my mom, yelling from the kitchen. "Telephone!"

Only one person ever calls me on the old-fashioned phone. Javier. His family moved here from Argentina last year. They still talk to their relatives there all the time, and I think when you make a call from here to Argentina (on a phone, not Skype), it's more expensive if you call a cell phone. I don't know for sure because I've never called Argentina. Anyway, Javier always calls me on the house phone.

I picked up the phone in my parents' room. That phone doesn't have a cord (the kitchen one does), so I could have brought it back to my room, but I like talking on the phone while I'm lying on my parents' bed. It's nice and big, and I can roll around.

Javier was calling to see if I want to play

football. The first time he did that I actually went. I like him, and people don't ask me to play football very often. It turned out he meant soccer, which I like a tiny bit more than football. Javier says I could be good at it because I run pretty fast and my feet are sort of big. Unfortunately, I just don't like it that much.

Javier is still learning English, and I don't speak Spanish (I take French), but I like talking to him. It's kind of like a word game. Part of the game is figuring out what he's trying to say, because he doesn't know certain words or he mixes them up or he says them in the wrong order.

The other part of the game is figuring out how to say things in English so he'll know what I'm saying. It's fun, but when you're on the phone, not looking at each other, not able to act things out, it's like you're playing the same game but you jumped to a higher level.

I said to Javier, "Unfortunately, I cannot play football because I am working on a very important project." I think it helps not to use contractions like "can't" or "I'm."

My mom walked in just as I was getting up. I started smoothing the covers, but I can never get it to look like it does when she makes the bed. Neither can my dad. She started smoothing the covers herself. "Why don't you invite Javier for dinner?"

"He's playing soccer."

"Then he'll be extra hungry."

"Are we having fish again?"

"No, Sean. I got the message. But I bet Javier loves fish."

I have no idea whether Javier loves or even likes fish, but anyway, I really want to get this agent thing taken care of. If we don't have a guest, dinner will be shorter and I can still make calls, because it's earlier in California, where most of the agents are.

On my way out I said, "Let's invite him another time. I have too much homework tonight." I don't like lying to my mom, but I actually didn't. What I have to do *is* work, and I'm doing it at home.

After dinner (lasagna), I tried getting in touch with some other agents. None of them wanted to talk to me. None of them even spent as much time telling me no as Delilah did.

Maybe I gave up on managers without knowing enough about them. I spent a little more time on the internet doing research. You know, not just Wikipedia.

Actually, Wikipedia isn't a bad place to start. I know Wikipedia isn't the total truth, but who says an encyclopedia in a regular library is the total truth?

When I was young, I had to do a report on Brazil. In the encyclopedia in my school library, the article about Brazil was exactly three pages long. Two hundred million people live in Brazil. It's a huge country, just a little bit smaller than all fifty United States. It's been around a long time. Are there really only three pages' worth of things to say about Brazil? Are those three pages the total truth about Brazil? No.

Here's what I learned online. Agents get 10 percent of what you earn. So if a big entertainment company pays you 10 million dollars for your idea, your agent gets 1 million and you get nine.

Managers get 15 percent. So if you have an agent and also a manager, out of that 10 million, you only get 7 1/2 million. For *your* idea. What do they even do?

According to what I read, agents and managers advise you. They negotiate the contract. They help guide your career. I guess I want those things. Even if I don't, I'm never going to get 10 million dollars from that big entertainment company for my idea if they won't even let me tell them what it is.

chapter 5

Seventh grade. What can you say? There's a law that says I have to go, so I go. I try to make the best of it, but some days that's not possible. Like today. I didn't feel like being in school, and I especially didn't feel like going to French, so I went to the Publication Room to pretend to work on the e-yearbook. I'm one of the editors.

I'm having a problem with my French teacher. It's really bothering me because I like French a lot, and this is making me not like it.

I like French because it's like a secret code. You see the words on a page, and not one single word sounds the way it looks. *Renseignement*. That means information. You could look at *renseignement* for a million years and you would never guess how to pronounce it. Only people who know the code know how to say it and only people who know the code know what you mean.

My mom speaks French. Sort of. She learned it in high school. She was always a very good student, and she knows the right way to say every single letter of the alphabet in French. Unfortunately, she pronounces every letter of every word so perfectly that it never actually sounds like a person talking.

You wouldn't think so if you met him, but my dad also speaks French. I only found out last year. My mom told me that my dad's family lived in Paris for a year when he was a kid. My dad never speaks French anymore because it reminds him of his dad. I never met that grandfather. He died before I was born. My dad is still mad at him about something.

Anyway, I really like speaking French, and I used to like French class. Last year my teacher, Mademoiselle Fou, decided she wanted to put on a show at our school. She set up the auditorium stage like a French nightclub, and kids from her classes were waiters, entertainers, or regular French people at the nightclub. There was a big sign over the stage that said LE BISTRO, which was the name of the nightclub and the name of the show.

She asked me to be the host because she said I have the best French accent in the school. I ended up spending a lot of time working on that show, and after a while it felt like too much time. Mademoiselle Fou is one of those teachers who tries to be friends with students. It's fun at first, then it isn't.

The real reason she did *Le Bistro* is that she likes to sing. She kept saying she was channeling Edith Piaf, a French singer who had a terrible life. I'm not sure what channeling is and none of us ever heard of Edith Piaf, but listening to Mademoiselle Fou sing songs in French at every rehearsal was giving *me* a terrible life.

I kept trying to help Mademoiselle Fou make the show better or even just shorter, but each time I made a suggestion, she would pat me on the head and say, *"Non, chéri."* ("No, sweetheart.")

The best thing about *Le Bistro* was meeting my

friend Brianna. She was in Mademoiselle Fou's other French class. For *Le Bistro*, Brianna thought up her own character, Dominique, a famous Paris fashion model. Every ten minutes during the show, the paparazzi (sixth graders) started flashing their cameras, and Dominique model-walked across the stage wearing sunglasses and different clothes. Then Mademoiselle Fou would come out and sing one more long song in French.

Here's some advice. If you don't like a show, don't tell the people in it that you liked it, or you'll probably have to sit through another one. People were really bored at *Le Bistro* last year, but everyone told Mademoiselle Fou it was good because they didn't know what else to say.

So of course there's going to be another *Le Bistro* this year. Brianna is going to New York next week to shop for outfits. I told Mademoiselle Fou I'm not going to do it this year. She didn't believe me for a long time, but now that she does, she's really mad.

She never calls on me in class, even when no one else knows the answer. She mostly stopped looking at me, which is good, because when she *does*, it's like I kicked her dog. She doesn't actually have a dog.

When I got to the Publication Room, there was no one else there, so I didn't have to pretend to work on the yearbook. I tried to figure out what to do about French. It's depressing. I decided to think about my career instead.

That's a little depressing too. Nothing is happening.

chapter 6

Managers don't have websites. Maybe they don't want people bothering them. People like me, I mean. Kind of like the agents. If you're not already famous, they're not going to try to make you famous.

I had to learn about managers from other websites. That's how I picked the manager I want. He manages Gina Gillespie (not her real name), an actress who is really, really good. She's completely different in each movie she's in. She's in a lot of movies, but she's not super-famous. Maybe because each time you see her, you think you never saw her before.

Maybe it's good that she's not so famous.

Because then you'd know all this extra stuff about her real life. And the next time you see her in a movie, you'll be thinking about all that extra stuff. She won't seem like a new character anymore. Just that actress who's the girlfriend of so-and-so. So I guess what I like about her manager is that Gina Gillespie keeps being in movies, and we don't know whose girlfriend she is.

I think about being famous. A lot, actually. There are some good things about it. If you're famous, you get to meet other famous people. It's like a big, fun club. It doesn't matter what you're famous for. You can automatically meet any other famous person you want to meet.

Look! There's a picture of the President, a football player, and a beautiful movie star. They're laughing together, with their arms around each other. What are they laughing at? What do they talk about when they're together? Being famous?

There are famous people I'd like to meet. I think. I've never met a famous person, so I don't actually know. I might want to wait until I'm famous myself. Because what could I say to them that wouldn't sound exactly the same as what everyone else who isn't famous says to them?

Maybe this manager can help me get the exact right amount of fame. And if I only have a manager, and not both an agent and a manager, I'll end up with 8 1/2 million out of the 10 million dollars for my idea. By the way, 10 million dollars is just a number I made up. I actually think my idea is worth much more than that.

So far, a letter didn't work and neither did phone calls, so this time I decided to try an e-mail. I don't use e-mail much. My grandmothers like it. They write these really long e-mails. You can tell that they're just kind of talking into the e-mail, and thinking that when I get it, I'll sit down and read the whole thing. I try to, but I always get distracted somewhere in the second or third paragraph.

I used to just stop when I got bored, but my grandmothers always ask me questions about things they say in their e-mails. So now I make myself read the whole thing, even it takes five tries.

And they have these crazy e-mail addresses.

My mom's mom is Mary Lou. Her e-mail address is MaryWho@_____.com. My dad's mom is ThornyRosen@_____.com. I think they think they're funny.

Martin Manager (not his real name) doesn't have a website. I looked for him on Facebook. I thought I'd recognize him because I saw a picture of him online with Gina Gillespie. He looks a little older than my parents.

One of the reasons I don't go on Facebook very often is that my one grandmother (Thorny) is constantly posting things. She's always mad about something, and we're all supposed to sign a petition or write a letter to complain. Or else she tells you really personal things. It's embarrassing. But maybe she thinks my podcasts are embarrassing.

Martin Manager isn't on Facebook. I used an online directory and got a phone number. I took a chance that it was actually him, and that it was his office and not his house. I called and asked for his e-mail address, and the guy who answered gave it to me. He probably thought I was a woman producer.

Dear Martin Manager,

I don't know you, but from what I read about you, I like the way you do things. I think you're doing an excellent job with Gina Gillespie.

I'm 13. Let's get that over with now. That's how old I am. I can't help it.

I want to work in the entertainment business. I want to make movies, TV shows, and probably plays. I also plan to get involved in music and games.

I have a big new idea that I want to work on with _____ (my first-choice entertainment company). I'm sure you know them better than I do.

If you think you might be interested in working with me, just send me an e-mail or call me at 555-555-5555.

Thanks,
Sean Rosen

Dear Martin Manager,

chapter 7

sent the e-mail. When you write an important e-mail, you can work on it for two hours, changing the words over and over again, then checking it eight times to see if you spelled everything right. But the minute you finally hit SEND, you think the other person got it, opened it, and is reading it right now.

I sat at my computer for a while, waiting for Martin Manager to reply. I know there are a million reasons why he might not drop everything and read my e-mail and get right back to me. Maybe he's having lunch with Gina Gillespie. Maybe he's out renting a tux for an awards show.

Even if he's just sitting there in his office and

he read it the minute he got it, he would still need a few minutes to figure out what he wants to say. I knew all that, but I couldn't stop staring at my inbox.

After ten minutes, I made myself do something else. I took a bike ride. I didn't bring my phone. I was taking this bike ride to stop thinking about whether I'm about to have a manager. If I had my phone, the whole time I was riding my bike I would hear it not ringing.

I ride my bike a lot, and we've always lived in this town, so sometimes it feels like my bike goes by itself and I can just sit there and think.

I don't know if this ever happens to you, but sometimes right before something big is going to happen, like you're starting a new school or you're getting a present you really want, you think, "Wow, things are really going to change. Today is the end of something. My life won't be like this ever again."

I was happy and sad at the same time. I want to get my career going, but there are also things I like about just being a kid.

I got home, and before I went upstairs to check my e-mail, I stopped in the kitchen to get something to drink. What I really wanted was lemonade right out of the carton. My mom doesn't like us (my dad and me) drinking from the carton if it's something that she or anyone else might ever want to drink. I was holding the carton, trying to decide what to do, when my mom walked in.

"Oh, good. Pour one for me, too." She had her hospital clothes on, and she looked pretty tired, so I didn't pretend to drink from the carton just to be funny. And I didn't try to convince her to do the pouring. Being a nurse seems like it's really tiring, but my mom likes it.

She thinks she and my dad have the easiest jobs of all their friends, because when they come home, they're done working. No one's texting them or e-mailing them all night. I know what she's saying, but I don't agree. My dad gets calls at the craziest times for plumbing emergencies. Someone was doing laundry at four in the morning and there was a flood. You'd be surprised how often that happens.

And some days when my mom takes care of someone who's really sick, she worries about them while she's at home. Sometimes she even calls the hospital to see how they're doing. I guess I can pour her a glass of lemonade.

I wanted to rush upstairs to see if Martin Manager wrote back, but I felt like the longer I could make myself wait, the better my chances were that he did. I have no idea if that's true. In a math way, I mean. I lasted about eighty seconds, then I ran upstairs.

I always go two steps at a time, but when I'm in a hurry, I think I can go three steps at a time. I can't. My mom heard the crash and yelled, "Are you okay?"

I can't believe it. He wrote back. It's so strange. It was the main thing I was thinking about, but I wasn't ready for it. I actually started shivering. This sounds crazy, but before I opened the e-mail, I took a picture of my inbox on the computer screen. Actually, it's a picture of me next to my inbox.

Then I thought about how I would feel if it was

just another stupid letter from a lawyer. If that happens, I'll delete the photo.

To: Sean Rosen
From: Martin Manager

Dear Sean,

You certainly write a good letter. I admire your ambition and your confidence. I'm not going to represent you right now, but I'll be watching the trades to see how you do with _____ (my first-choice company).

As you proceed, if you have a specific business question I might be able to answer, try me.

Best,
Martin

Wow. He's telling me no, but I actually feel great. I feel like this is all going to work out. In case you don't know, when he said he'd be watching the trades, he meant he'd be looking in *The*

Hollywood Reporter and *Variety* to see if there's an article about me and my idea. *Variety* is the other show business magazine. I'd get them both, but they're very expensive. *The Hollywood Reporter* has more pages and more pictures.

That's so cool that he just signed it "Martin." Like we're already friends. And that he ended the e-mail with "Best." He didn't say Best what, but I like the way it sounds.

I'm not going to e-mail him again until I have a really important question. But it's so great that he said I can. And he said he won't represent me right now, but he didn't say not ever. He didn't even say not soon.

Obviously, I'm not going to delete the photo I took.

I decided to take the rest of the day off from trying to get an agent or a manager. You know, to celebrate. Plus, I have to get to work on my podcast. I recorded it last Saturday at a donut place, but I still have to finish the song, and editing takes hours and hours and hours if you want to get it right.

You can start working on it right after dinner, and the next time you look, it's ten o'clock. Or eleven. Or twelve. Time goes really fast. It's like the opposite of school.

I could tell you about my podcast, and maybe sometime I will, but it's better if you just take a look. If I tell you about it, you'll imagine what it's going to be like. Then when you finally see it, you'll just compare what you imagined to what it actually is. Here's one you might like: www.SeanRosen.com/hair.

This week's podcast is a little more complicated than usual. Someone said something in her interview that I think she might not want everyone in the world to hear. I'm not saying that everyone in the world watches my podcasts, but they can. Anyway, I don't want to get her in trouble.

She said something about the donut place that isn't very nice. I went back to ask her if it's okay if I use her interview. I brought it with me so she could hear it. People sometimes forget they said certain things.

She wasn't there. She doesn't work there

anymore. I guess either she or her boss figured out that she didn't like her job. I decided not to use her interview.

I finished editing a few minutes before midnight. My parents don't like me staying up that late on a school night, but when I turned thirteen they said, "We're not going to be the Bedtime Police anymore." I'm happy with the podcast. It makes me want a donut, but I'm too tired to get one.

chapter 8

Something funny happened at school today. It was about halfway through history. Some years I like history, but this year is really boring. You won't believe it, but Mr. Knapp, my history teacher, was also my mom's history teacher. I guess he wasn't all that interesting back then either. She calls him "The Appropriately Named Mr. Knapp."

I was looking out the window thinking how cool it was that Martin Manager said I write a good letter, when I heard, "Sean Rosen!" From the way he said my name, it was probably the second or third time. "Perhaps we could interrupt your reverie to hear your assessment of the failures of Reconstruction."

I tried reading that chapter last night after I finished my podcast. I started it and I woke up with the book on my chest. I didn't even make it through the first paragraph. "Yes. The failures . . . The failures of Reconstruction. Well . . . "

Just then a light started flashing and a very annoying buzzer started buzzing. Fire drill! Or who knows, maybe a real fire. Right then I didn't care which. Mr. Knapp didn't look happy. "Perhaps Mr. Rosen will share some of his vast knowledge when we return."

We walked single-file out of the classroom. Javier was right in front of me. We're not supposed to talk during a fire drill, but everyone does. "Javi, do you know?"

"No, mi amigo."

We got outside and stood on the grass. We're not supposed to take anything with us, but Brianna had her bag. "Like I'm gonna leave a Prada bag sitting in a classroom."

I asked Brianna if she knew about the failures of Reconstruction. She pulled out her phone. It's some kind of superphone that's still being beta tested. She typed something in, waited one second, then pushed a button and out came a little piece of paper. She handed it to me.

FAILURES OF RECONSTRUCTION
- Status of former slaves didn't improve.
- Economy of South didn't recover.
- Division between North and South didn't heal.

Then we heard a long, loud beep. The fire drill was over. The assistant principal came on the loudspeaker. "Evacuation time: three minutes and twenty-six seconds. If this had been a real fire, we could have had some badly burned students. We can do better, people." She definitely doesn't want us to burn, but she also wants to break the county record.

By the time we were back in our seats, I had the Failures of Reconstruction memorized. Mr. Knapp was just about to call on me when Mademoiselle Fou stuck her head into the classroom.

What is *she* doing here? Is this some kind of meeting of the Sean Rosen Non-Fan Club? They stood near the door and kept whispering to each other. Break it up! We're trying to learn some history here!

Then the bell rang. Oh well.

When I got home, I changed. I don't care much about clothes, but after wearing something all day at school, I want to feel like I'm not there anymore. I have history homework, and since we probably won't have another fire drill tomorrow, I better do it. Soon. But not yet.

I can't stop thinking about sending another e-mail to Martin Manager. He's my only friend in show business. I know, he's not exactly my friend. But compared to everyone else, he is.

I'm not sure if anyone else does this, but sometimes I practice what I'm going to say to someone. Like if I'm nervous about it. I don't actually say it out loud. I just say it in my head. Then I keep going over and over it. I don't want to, but I can't stop.

I know I shouldn't write to Martin until I have something important to say. And after hearing what I was going to say about 600 times, I was sure it wasn't important.

I don't know what to do next. You'd think that getting such a quick answer from Martin Manager would make me want to try another manager, but it doesn't. If I'm going to have a manager, I want Martin.

When my Dad came home from work, he said, "Seany . . . I met a guy who knows a guy who might be able to help you."

Someone whose toilet my dad fixed has a brother-in-law who's a producer. One of the things my dad loves about his job is that he gets to work with all kinds of people. "That's the beauty of it, Seany. Sooner or later in life, everybody needs a plumber."

My dad didn't ask the producer's name, so I couldn't Google him. But the guy with the toilet said his brother-in-law is always looking for projects.

A project is show-business language for anything you're trying to get started—a movie, a TV show, a book. My idea, the one I want to work on with my first-choice company, isn't actually a project. It's more like an idea you would use on a lot of different projects. I don't think there's a show-business name yet for my kind of idea.

So even though I don't exactly have a project and I'm not exactly looking for a producer, my dad was so excited about helping me that I let him plan a meeting for me with this guy whose name he doesn't know.

chapter 9

Here's what happened at my first show-business meeting. It was a few days later at a restaurant. My dad drove me there in his van. The producer and I went to a table near the back. My dad sat at the counter.

I wasn't sure if the producer noticed my digital voice recorder on the table. It kind of looks like a phone, especially when it's upside down and you can't see the red light that tells you it's recording.

PRODUCER: So you're the little genius.
ME: Um . . . I'm not exactly
           little.

PRODUCER: Don't fight it, kid. It's your
          gimmick. Work it. In fact,
          can we say you're twelve?
ME: No. Say it to who?
PRODUCER: Whoever we pitch to.

"Pitching" in show-business language means telling someone about your project so they'll want to buy it.

WAITRESS: What can I get you two?
PRODUCER: Coffee. Black.
ME: I'll have a chocolate shake.
PRODUCER: You know how to live.

The waitress left.

ME: What have you actually
          produced?
PRODUCER: Movies, TV, you name it.
ME: Um . . . Why don't *you* name
          it. I mean the things you
          produced.

PRODUCER: Cocky little kid. I like it.

He named three things I never heard of.

ME: Have you worked with any of the really big companies?

PRODUCER: Trust me, they're all the same. So what's your idea?

ME: Really? You want to work with me?

PRODUCER: I'm here, aren't I?

ME: Why? I'm your brother-in-law's plumber's son.

PRODUCER: This is what producers do. We look for projects.

ME: How many projects do you have?

PRODUCER: Who the hell knows? Does it matter?

ME: Like three? Like thirty?

PRODUCER: Between three and thirty. You're worse than the IRS.

The waitress brought his coffee and my shake.

ME: Do you have a lot of people working for you?

PRODUCER: A lot? No. Most of the time you're just waiting. Waiting for someone to read a script. Waiting for someone to come up with the money.

ME: Speaking of money, how does that work?

PRODUCER: Tell me your idea, and I'll lay it all out for you.

ME: If I tell you my idea, do you pay me?

PRODUCER: Are you kidding me? You should pay me. I'm the guy with the connections. But I'll take this on out of the goodness of my heart. When I sell it, you'll get paid.

ME:	How much?
PRODUCER:	I don't know. I don't even know what we're talking about here. What's this big idea?
ME:	An agent gets 10 percent. A manager gets 15 percent. What do you get?
PRODUCER:	You're very suspicious, kid. It's kind of a turnoff. Don't worry about me. You'll get yours and I'll get mine.

I never told him my idea. He didn't want to pay for my shake, but he did.

I decided not to play the recording of the meeting for my dad. I don't want him to feel bad. I know he was happy he could help me meet this producer, but he wasn't surprised I don't want to work with him.

"To tell you the truth, Seany, that guy seemed a little oily." I wasn't sure what that meant, but he did have very shiny hair. I told my dad that the producer said he would work with me out of the goodness of his heart. My dad said, "That clinches it. If his heart was any good, he wouldn't say that. I should've charged his brother-in-law more for the toilet."

chapter 10

I know I complain about school, but there *is* one class I like. English is almost always fun for me. I like to read and I like to write, and we have a very fun English teacher this year.

Miss Meglis LOVES her job. She loves almost every book we read, and if she doesn't, she loves talking about why not. She's young and she has so much energy that I wish I had *her* after lunch, instead of . . . yawn . . . snore. . . . Sorry. I took a Knapp just thinking about him.

"Okay, laddies and lassies . . ." (We just finished a book that takes place in Ireland.) "For Wednesday, you, working in teams of two, will pick up where the author left off."

In the book, a brother and sister are separated when they're little, and they finally find each other again in the last chapter.

"I know we were all rooting for this reunion, but real life is complicated. What do you think took place the day *after* the book ended? Each team will write a short scene and act it out for the edification and gratification of the class."

She loves to make us look up words.

I usually hate working on group projects. I hate the part where you pick the people you're going to work with. I hate deciding who's going to do what. I hate worrying if the other people are actually going to do what they're supposed to. I hate when I don't like what they did. I never know what to do. Should I try to fix it? If I don't fix it, will the teacher blame *me* for the parts I hate?

It's a little better when it's just two people. Brianna and I figured out how we like to work together. You wouldn't think the two of us would even get along. We're so different. She always looks perfect, and I look like . . . well . . . me.

Brianna and I went to different elementary

schools. That's why we didn't meet until *Le Bistro*. Where we live, there's one part of town where all the big expensive houses are. That's where Brianna lives. And that's where we had our meeting yesterday for this English project.

Brianna's house is huge. I always get lost when I'm there, and there's never anyone around to ask directions. Her dad travels a lot, and her mom is either out or in some part of the house I've never been to. One of her brothers lives there, but you never see him. I think he has his own entrance. The other brother refuses to live in the house. He has an apartment somewhere.

Brianna offered me a snack. I was hungry, but I don't like the food they have there. It's all either diet or healthy. She had some kind of green juice and rice cakes. No thanks.

Brianna said, "Did you read the book?"

"Yeah. Did you?"

"Mostly. Remind me how it ends."

"Really?"

"Come on, Sean, I only have an hour. Let's not waste time. Do you have an idea?"

"I do, actually."

"Good. Do you want to write it?"

"Yeah."

"Do you want me to help?"

"Not really."

"Okay. Tell me when you're done."

We sat there together. I wrote the scene for the brother and sister, and Brianna texted with her friends. She has a lot of friends, and each time she got a text, I forgot what I was writing.

"Can you turn off the sound on that thing?"

She looked at me for a second. "Only for you, Sean." Brianna doesn't like people to tell her what to do, which is something we have in common. But she thinks I'm creative, so when it comes to things like this, she listens to me.

Brianna was actually the first person to see one of my podcasts. She says she loves them. I don't tell many people at my school about my podcasts. They're not about school, and I'm sure some kids would think they're weird or stupid. I don't want to have to hear about it.

Anyway, I finished the scene, we rehearsed

it on the phone last night, and in class today, Brianna and I were about to start acting out our scene when the door opened. Everyone suddenly got very quiet. This gigantic kid walked in and handed Miss Meglis a note.

"Everybody, let's welcome Ethan Rodgers to our class. Ethan's family just moved here. Would you like to tell us a little about yourself?"

It got very quiet again. Ethan didn't say a word. He just sat down in an empty seat in the back. I tried not to stare at him like everyone else did. He's huge. You would never believe he's a seventh grader. He's taller than any teacher in the school, and he's not just tall. He's big. Big shoulders, big arms, big legs.

Brianna and I read our scene. I thought the day after the end of the book would be a little sad but also funny. The brother and sister are happy to be back together, but each of them thinks the other is annoying. I noticed that Ethan was the only one who got some of the jokes.

I kind of wish Brianna had read more of the book, because she wasn't acting anything like the sister. She was exactly like Brianna. The second we were done, Mr. Obester, the phys ed teacher, walked into the classroom. I think he was standing outside waiting for us to finish.

"Miss Meglis, excuse me for one minute." Then he looked around until he found Ethan, which wasn't too hard. "Ethan, I stopped by to personally welcome you to the school. I'm hoping you'll come out for the football team."

For some kids this would be the greatest day of their life, but Ethan looked really uncomfortable. He didn't say anything. "Or maybe basketball is your game." Ethan still didn't say anything. "Or wrestling." The classroom was very quiet. Finally, Ethan said something. "No."

Mr. Obester left. I don't know if Ethan isn't good at sports or if he just doesn't want to be on a team, but the way he said "No" it sounded like the final answer.

The bell rang. Ethan looked relieved and I was glad, too. There was no time to talk about our scene, which was just okay, not great. It wasn't really Brianna's fault. But it reminded me how much I want to start working with professionals.

chapter 11

After school, I went to the public library to do a little more research. I like libraries. They're sort of like museums.

I never knew this, but there's actually a whole section of books on how to be successful in show business. You know, how to write a screenplay, how to win an Oscar. They make it sound so easy. Just follow these steps and you will be famous. I doubt it.

I found out something interesting about producers. According to one of the books, anyone in the world can call himself a producer. You don't have to do anything first. You just start telling people you're a producer.

I produce my podcasts. I actually *am* a producer.

But even if I wasn't, even if I never produced anything, I could still tell you I'm the President of Sean Rosen Productions.

I don't want to be that kind of producer. I don't want to be like the producer I met at the restaurant. After our meeting, I looked him up online and I never heard of any of the things he produced or any of the people he worked with.

I know it sounds like the only thing I care about is whether or not people are famous. That's not true. There are some famous people who aren't very talented. I never want to work with them. There are some talented people who aren't even a tiny bit famous (um . . . me?). But I do want a lot of people to see my work, and most of the time that only happens if someone famous is involved.

Remember the letter from the legal department at my trial run company? I put it in the bottom of a drawer, so I wouldn't have to see it. When I got home from the library, I looked at it again.

It's still annoying, but that letter doesn't make me feel bad anymore. It still says I shouldn't have written to them. It still says that my idea is probably like fifty other ideas they already own. (It isn't.) But now, even though the letter has my name and address at the top, and it says "Dear Mr. Rosen," I know they weren't really talking to me. They don't know me. They don't know my idea. It's just the letter they send to anyone who writes to them.

"Should you wish to approach this company again, we suggest that you do so through a talent agent or management firm."

I wonder if agents and managers are like producers. Can anyone just start saying they're an agent or a manager?

My dad offered to be my agent. Here's what he would tell people: "Seany's pretty good. But you better do everything you say you're gonna do, because if you don't, you won't wanna be around him." Thanks, Dad. It's true, I guess.

People are curious about my dad. Most people don't know any Jewish plumbers. I guess most plumbers have fathers and grandfathers who were also plumbers. My dad had a father who wore a tie every day and worked in a nice office. I don't know much about it, but I know things didn't turn out so great for Grandpa.

I already told my dad I'm not going into the plumbing business with him. He laughed and said, "I know, Seany." Anyway, he's not going to be my agent.

I went online and found out that even if I wanted him to be, my dad *can't* be my agent. He doesn't have a license. Well, he does, but it's a plumbing license. My mom actually has a license, too. I understand why you want your nurse or your plumber to have a license. You want to know they went to school and they know what they're doing.

I guess you want your agent to know what he's doing, too. Since none of the agents with licenses will even talk to me, I started thinking about managers again, because managers don't need a license.

I remember when I started out, I sat around deciding what I wanted—an agent or a manager or both. I actually thought they would all want to work with me.

When you're sitting alone at home with your idea, you imagine the finished thing that everyone is going to see. You don't know all the things you have to do to get to the finished thing.

The other part I never thought about when I started was how it sounds when you tell someone you have an amazing idea. Probably everyone thinks their own ideas are amazing. No offense, but a lot of them aren't.

That's why it's good to hear from another person that something is great. That's what my manager can do. And even though people will know he works for me, it's a lot better than hearing *me* say it.

"Sean! Dinner. Now."

I was on my way downstairs when I heard my phone. I knew I shouldn't but I went back to see who it was. It was a text from Brianna.

I'm going to kill my mother.

I couldn't help it. I had to text her back.

While you're in prison, can I have your phone?

chapter 12

French today was all about *Le Bistro*. We watched the video from last year. I was actually pretty good, but the show was embarrassing. When the bell rang, I tried to hurry out, but Mademoiselle Fou stopped me. *"Eh bien?"* ("Well?")

"I'm sorry. I can't this year. I'm in the middle of something outside of school." Which is completely true. She looked at me and made a French sound that if you could translate it would mean, "I doubt it. I despise you. Get out of my classroom."

When I got home from school, I went right upstairs. No snack. No anything. This is serious. I have to figure this out. How am I going to get a manager?

I kept thinking about Martin Manager. I wonder if I can beg him, in some way that doesn't sound like begging. But he's smart. He would recognize begging.

I don't like begging people to do things. Then if they say yes, they're doing you this huge favor, and you both know it. You feel like you have to keep thanking them the whole time, and they sort of want you to. I want someone who actually *wants* to work with me.

I decided to try writing the letter I would want my manager to send to the huge entertainment company I want to work with.

Dear _____, (an important person at the company)

I'm writing to tell you about my newest client. I think you two could do amazing work together.

Sean Rosen is not only my newest client. He's my youngest. At thirteen, he's already an experienced writer and producer. I encourage you to watch some of Sean's podcasts (www.SeanRosen.com). They're uniquely entertaining.

Sean has an idea that I honestly think will blow you away. Your company is his first choice, and I would love for the two of you to get to know each other.

I really think there's something special here, or I wouldn't waste your time with this.

Best,

_____ (the manager I don't have)

I kept reading the letter. I like it. It doesn't sound like me. It sounds a little like Mr. Hollander, a math teacher at my school. I don't have him for math, but he's the advisor for the e-yearbook.

Could Mr. Hollander be my manager? He's a good guy. He isn't afraid to tell you he likes your work. And you believe him because he tells you exactly what he likes about it. When he told me I was going to be an editor this year, he actually said, "I'm a fan."

But even if Mr. Hollander ever wanted to be

my manager, I don't really want this to be a school thing. Like I said, I don't love school. So why am I a yearbook editor? It's fun, it gets me out of classes sometimes, and it helps me pretend that I don't *go* to that school. I'm just working on a *book* about that school.

Maybe my mom's friend Debbie could be my manager. My mom knows her from when they were in sixth grade. They love to tell me that for some reason.

Debbie never stops working. She sometimes pretends she's relaxing, like on a weekend, but she never is. I don't feel sorry for her. She actually likes working all the time. I want a manager who works as hard as Debbie does.

But Debbie can't be my manager. She's known me since I was born. She always brings up things I might not want everyone in the world to know. I'm thirteen years old and she's still telling the diaper story.

I read the letter again. What if instead of a blank line at the bottom, it had a name. A name I made up.

I pictured the important person at the big company getting it. Let's say he's the Vice President of New Projects. I don't know if there's actually a job called that, but let's say there is and he gets this letter. He would probably think, "Whoever this Sean Rosen is, he must be good if he's only thirteen and he already has a manager who really believes in him."

Then he would think, "But I never heard of this manager." Then he would think, "But with a company as big as mine, and all these projects I'm in charge of, how can I know every single manager?" Managers don't have websites, so if you got an e-mail from a manager you didn't know, you wouldn't be able to find out much about him. Or her.

Maybe I can have an imaginary manager.

Maybe I can. I like the way he writes letters.

I guess he's a he.

What would he need? Just an e-mail address. No one really calls anyone anymore, except when they're bored.

I can get him an e-mail address. Anyone can

get an e-mail address. I have two. I only use one of them. The first one got so crowded with e-mails that I stopped going there. It was my fault. Every time a website asked for my e-mail address to send me "special offers only available online," I gave it to them.

Okay, I'll get him an e-mail account. What should his e-mail address be? Sean'sManager@_____.com? No. That sounds like I have a thirteen-year-old manager.

Maybe just his name. What is his name?

I went to the kitchen. Maybe I can get some ideas there. Or at least something to eat. I stood in front of the refrigerator. It's pretty full. Everyone in my family likes to eat, and whenever someone is near a store they call whoever's home to see what we need. I'm glad we do that. Some people, even people who have a lot of money, never have any food in the house.

I'm hungry, but I don't know what I want. There's a bowl of little carrots, so I started eating them while I looked for something better. I don't mind carrots, but no matter how hard you try, you can't pretend they're potato chips. I looked around the refrigerator to see if there are any good names for my manager. Kraft Tropicana? No. Heinz Dannon? No. Dannon Heinz? That's not bad. I like the first name Dannon. He would say, "Yes. Like the yogurt. You can call me Dan."

I'm not sure about Heinz. I looked in some cabinets. Now I want potato chips, but unfortunately we don't have any. What else could his name be? Dannon Pepperidge? No. Dannon Ronzoni? No. I went back to the refrigerator.

Dan Welch. Not Dannon, just Dan. Dan Welch. "Yes. Like the grape juice." *Best, Dan Welch.* I like it.

I ran back upstairs. My e-mail company already has a DanWelch. They say that DanWelch7 is available. I don't think my manager wants anyone to think he's the seventh anything. Dan.Welch? Someone has it. I tried DanWelchManagement. It's available. We grabbed it.

Wait a minute. I just said "we." "We," as in me and Dan. Dan and me. Dan and I? Whatever, he's only been around for a half hour, and Dan Welch already feels like a real person. A real person with an e-mail address.

Did you ever hear someone say, "I'm going to sleep on it"? It's like deciding not to decide something until the next day. It was tempting to use Dan's e-mail address right away, but this idea is so weird that I thought I should sleep on it.

chapter 13

woke up feeling good. I have a manager. I don't know why, but I actually believe it. It was even a good day at school. Until lunchtime.

There's nothing I like about my school cafeteria. I don't like the way it looks, I don't like the way it smells, I don't like how noisy it is. And the food? No.

I avoid going there. Sometimes I go to the Publication Room (it helps to be an editor). Sometimes I volunteer to help Trish, the principal's assistant. I have a few other hiding places around school that I can't tell you about, because they only fit one person.

I bring my own lunch. My dad or my mom used

to put my lunch together for me, and they're both actually good at it. I got some ideas from them, but now I like to do it myself. I made a really good lunch today. A perfect peanut butter and jelly sandwich, a little bag of pretzels, the exact drink I wanted, the cookie I wanted, and an orange, which makes my whole lunch bag smell good.

After a morning of half paying attention to geometry and earth science and half thinking about Dan Welch, I couldn't wait to bite into that sandwich. I opened my locker and I didn't see my lunch bag. I don't have the world's neatest locker, so it took me a minute to be absolutely sure it wasn't in there somewhere. But then I hit ◄◄ in my brain, and I saw how I forgot it.

Right as I was leaving the house, I got this crazy thought. "What if someone already wrote to Dan Welch?" No one but me ever heard of Dan Welch. No one has his e-mail address. I was already late. Still, I ran up the stairs (missed one, crashed), checked Dan Welch's e-mail, saw the number "3" in the inbox, got excited, opened the inbox, found three "Welcome!" e-mails from the e-mail company, looked at the clock, saw how late I was *now*, ran out of the house, and left my lunch sitting on the kitchen counter.

I'm hungry! I want my delicious lunch! I felt like crying, but I was standing next to my locker in a busy hallway. I actually don't mind crying. What I don't like is crying in front of other people. Or when other people cry in front of me. You never know what to do.

Anyway, I didn't cry. I went to the cafeteria. Unfortunately, it was exactly like I remembered it.

One of the cafeteria ladies recognized me. She might have been one of the den mothers when I was in the Cub Scouts for two months. She gave me an extra big piece of something they're calling "pizza."

I paid, then I walked out and looked around the room. Brianna had a big table of girls listening to her. She saw me and waved. I looked down at the "pizza" and made a funny face.

I saw a table where Ethan, the new kid, was sitting by himself. I walked over and he looked down at the table.

"Okay if I sit here?"

First, he shrugged, kind of like, "I don't decide who sits where in this place." Then he sort of nodded, like, "It's a free country. If you want to sit here, sit here." But not in a mean way.

"Okay. Thanks."

Ethan didn't say anything the whole time. I didn't either. I actually like it that way. I eat lunch by myself most days, so I'm used to it being quiet. The cafeteria was as noisy as usual, but not our table. The pizza wasn't as gross as it looked. Lunch actually turned out okay.

When I got home, I put Dan Welch's name at the bottom of the letter to my first-choice company.

Dear _____, (an important person at the huge company)

I'm writing to tell you about my newest client. I think you two could do amazing work together.

Sean Rosen is not only my newest client. He's my

youngest. At thirteen, he's already an experienced writer and producer. I encourage you to watch some of Sean's podcasts (www.SeanRosen.com). They're uniquely entertaining.

Sean has an idea that I honestly think will blow you away. Your company is his first choice, and I would love for the two of you to get to know each other.

I really think there's something special here, or I wouldn't waste your time with this.

Best,
Dan

I think he would sign it Dan, not Dan Welch. Because they're both in the big family of show business, and even if you don't know someone, you sort of do. Or that's how they act when they meet each other on talk shows.

I'm not sure if I even want to say what it felt like to read this letter from Dan Welch, because you'll think I'm crazy. I mean actually crazy. But here goes. It felt amazing to read it, because it feels like someone really believes in me.

Tell the truth. You think I'm crazy, right? If you told me this same story about you and your own Dan Welch, I guarantee I would think you were crazy. I'd say, "Dude. You *are* Dan Welch. *You* wrote that letter." I actually never call anyone "Dude," but maybe I would this time because I'd want you to know how completely crazy I think you are.

I can't really explain it, but I'm not Dan Welch. And he isn't me.

I went to my website and added a sentence: For all business questions, please contact Dan Welch. Then if you click on the name Dan Welch, it opens your e-mail program and automatically puts in his e-mail address so you can write to him. I wonder if anyone ever will.

I only have my one big idea (so far), and before going to my first-choice company with it, Dan Welch is doing his own trial run. And just for fun, he's going to the same company I wrote to when I started—the one with the lawyers.

I Googled the company and found an article

where they say the name of someone who's Vice President of Production. I called the company and got her e-mail address.

To: Stefanie V. President (not her real name)
From: Dan Welch Management

Dear Stefanie,

A new client of mine, Sean Rosen, a thirteen-year-old if you can believe it, has an amazing idea for a movie. It might even be a series of movies. I've never heard anything like it. It's totally original. Any interest?

Best,
Dan

I know we don't want to tell the trial run company my big idea, but I wonder why Dan said I have an idea for a movie. I actually don't. I will at some point, I'm sure. I'm glad he thinks I can do it.

I hit SEND and suddenly got very nervous.

What if they know? What if they recognize my name from my first letter? Maybe I'm on some kind of list. "Here are the people who have made trouble for us. If you see any of these names, DO NOT REPLY. Just call the legal department."

Or maybe their company has an e-mail program that automatically recognizes the names on The Troublemaker List, and instead of sending Dan Welch's e-mail about me to Stefanie V. President, it goes directly to the legal department, with a copy to the police.

But wait a minute. That's the same legal department who told me that if I want to submit something, I have to do it through an agent or a manager. That's exactly what I'm doing. More or less.

chapter 14

We have to go to my cousin Jakey's bar mitzvah this weekend. It's in Detroit. At dinner tonight I asked my parents if I could skip it, and they both looked at me like I was crazy. I knew they wouldn't let me stay home by myself. And I knew they wouldn't let me miss Jakey's bar mitzvah.

Now I wish I didn't even ask. Now they have to think, "Sean doesn't want to be there." They probably already knew that, but the nice thing would be to pretend I wanted to go.

Unfortunately, I'm a terrible pretender. A lot of the time I don't even try. If I try, I get mad that I have to pretend. Then I'm mad that I have to be there, plus I'm mad that I have to pretend I want to be there. It's not much fun for anyone.

The reason I want to skip the bar mitzvah has nothing to do with my cousin. I like Jakey. I just don't like going to bar mitzvahs. Or weddings. Or sweet-sixteen parties. I don't like when people come up and light candles on a cake for a half hour. I don't like when they carry people around on chairs. I don't like finding a card with my name on it telling me where I have to sit.

I didn't have a bar mitzvah. My mom was into it for a little while. She isn't even the Jewish one. I think she was trying to do something to make my grandmother (Thorny Rosen) happy. After my mom figured out that I really didn't want one, and that my dad really didn't care, she let it go. But she made my dad tell my grandmother.

It was nothing against the religion. I like being partially Jewish. What I didn't want was the whole thing of everyone acting a whole lot nicer to you than usual. Everyone. Relatives you don't really know, friends of your parents you don't even like, and all these kids suddenly paying all this attention to you. Everyone watching you. It's too weird.

After dinner, I went up to my bedroom and slid under my bed. There's a space between the rug and the mattress where it's dark and you have to lie flat. It's a good place to think. I think I should go downstairs and apologize.

When I got to the top of the stairs, my mom was on the bottom, on her way up. We both stopped and looked at each other. Who was going to go first?

"Mom . . . I'm sorry. You know . . . about what I said. You know . . . about not going to Jakey's bar mitzvah."

"Thank you."

"I'm gonna go."

"I know you are. But I have an idea."

"You do?"

"Yes. Don't sound so surprised. I just called Aunt Sandy, and it's okay with them if you want to . . . "

"What? Light a candle?"

"No, Sean. Everyone knows. You hate the

candles. She said it's okay if you do your podcast there."

"At the bar mitzvah?"

She nodded. I walked down to the step where we're the same height. "Mom . . . You're a genius."

She is. It's perfect. I immediately had a million ideas for a bar mitzvah podcast. Now I can't wait.

We flew to Detroit on Friday. My dad planned it so we would land a half hour before my grandmother (Thorny). That way we'd have time to get the rental car, and when Grandma arrives, we'll be all ready to go. We'll drop her at the hotel, then drive to the house where we're staying with friends of my cousins.

Unfortunately, my dad is a plumber, not an air traffic controller. Our plane landed a half-hour *after* Grandma's.

When we were finally on the ground, he called her on the phone he made her get. She didn't answer. We looked in baggage claim, but she wasn't there. He got the airport to make an announcement, but she didn't pick up a white courtesy phone. Even if you heard that announcement, *what's* a white courtesy phone, and where do you pick it up?

My mom kept making suggestions, but my dad wasn't in the mood for suggestions. He decided to get the rental car taken care of. When we got to Budget, Grandma was there renting a car.

"I wasn't going to wait forever. And frankly, I'd rather have my own car." Grandma hates the way my dad drives and my dad hates the way Grandma drives.

"No way. You're not driving at night. You don't know Detroit. We don't need two cars. Why do you *never* answer your phone?"

That was the last thing I heard because I put my earbuds in and listened to music until everybody calmed down. It only took two songs. She would never admit it, but I'm sure Grandma is relieved she doesn't have to drive.

The podcast kept me busy all weekend, which was good, because I wasn't thinking about Dan Welch the whole time. Like wondering if Stefanie V. President wrote back to him. Or if she hired an internet detective to find out who he is. Or if the internet detective figured out that it's me. Or if there's going to be a police car in front of our house when we get back from Detroit. I guess I did think about all those things, but mostly at night, in bed.

I didn't check e-mail the whole time we were there. Our cousins' friends kept asking me if I wanted to use a computer. They had five computers for four people. I don't like people to use my computer, so I didn't use theirs. I don't want to feel guilty if they ever come to our house.

At the synagogue, I sat between my dad and Grandma. It's good to keep those two separated. Every once in a while I recorded part of the service for my podcast. As soon as she saw the red light go on, Grandma would lean over and whisper something right into my digital voice recorder. "He's doing a marvelous job." "She wore *that* to a synagogue?" "Don't you wish *you* had a bar mitzvah?" Grandma is not a quiet whisperer.

The big party was at night at the hotel where Grandma was staying. In the afternoon a bus was taking the kids to play laser tag. I didn't want to, but I thought about going anyway, just for the podcast. Then I thought about laser tag. It's too dark for pictures, and it sounds like a video game with a lot of kids yelling. No.

My dad wanted to drive around Detroit. I didn't want to. Neither did Grandma, though she said she would if she could drive. She and I went for a walk instead. I had my digital voice recorder in my pocket. I decided it would be a more natural conversation if she didn't know she was being recorded.

GRANDMA: Sean, I'm glad you don't go for those violent games.

ME: Laser tag?

GRANDMA: What isn't violent about pointing a gun at someone?

ME: You're just trying to score points.

GRANDMA: By shooting each other. It's terrible. I think it's the schools. They don't teach you values anymore.

ME: When was the last time you were in a school?

Only my grandmother could get me to stick up
for laser tag and school, two things I don't even like.

GRANDMA: That's not the point. I
           live with the products of
           our schools. Salespeople
           who won't look you in the
           eye. Drivers who veer into
           your lane because they're
           at the wheel sexting.
ME: I think you mean texting.
GRANDMA: You've got an answer for
           everything, don't you? Well,
           tell me this . . . Do you
           know one kid who doesn't
           want to be rich?

I thought about it.

ME: Actually, no. But what's
           wrong with being rich?
GRANDMA: Plenty of things. Plenty of
           things.

I thought about it some more.

ME: **I don't want to be rich just to be rich. But if my career turns out the way I want it to, and millions of people are enjoying my movies and TV shows and games, I just <u>will</u> be rich. I actually don't think there's anything wrong with that.**

She didn't say anything. She just gave me a really strong hug. Grandma is a fierce hugger. It actually hurts.

When we got back to the hotel, I noticed there was a computer in the lobby. I thought about quickly checking Dan Welch's e-mail, but whatever might be there . . .

a) nothing

b) an e-mail to Dan from Stefanie V. President

c) an e-mail saying the Dan Welch account is closed because there actually *is* no Dan Welch. . .

I didn't want to find out in a hotel lobby. Plus, my parents were back from their drive, and we had to go change for the party.

The party was crazy. Jakey couldn't decide on a theme, so he had two. One was Las Vegas, so there was gambling, and waitresses in very small, very sparkly costumes. The other theme was the Detroit Red Wings, so the waiters all wore hockey uniforms. One of the waiters tripped on his skates and knocked over a waitress and her tray of drinks. I didn't see it (I heard it), but one of Jakey's friends told me the waitress's top came off for a few seconds.

You could have your picture taken in front of an actual hockey goal with an actual Detroit Red Wing. I forget which one. Obviously, there was a lot of good stuff for my podcast.

chapter 15

When we got home, there wasn't a police car waiting for me. We went inside and I unpacked. I hate packing for a trip. My mom tries to help me, but she gives up after about five minutes. Unpacking is easy. Everything either goes in the laundry or back in the closet because you didn't wear it or it isn't that dirty.

I started up my annoying computer. It's almost three years old, and when you first turn it on, it takes forever. I usually just leave it on, but we were going away. If I started it before unpacking, it would be ready by now.

I decided to play Ricochet Roulette while I waited. It's a game I made up. It actually has nothing to do with roulette, but I like the name. The only equipment you need is a beach ball, the kind that floats in the air, that you blow up. You lay on your bed on your back. You try to hit the ball up to the ceiling four times, without ever letting it touch the bed or the floor. That's the easy part.

In each game, you can only touch the ball once with each arm or leg. So if you hit it the first time with your right arm, when the ball comes down, you have to hit it with a leg or your left arm. Sometimes you fall off the bed trying to hit the ball with your left leg, after you already used up both arms and your right leg.

It sounds complicated, but it really isn't. The trick is to not hit the ball too hard. Tonight I played three times and won twice.

I went to the Dan Welch Management e-mail account. I could have had Dan Welch's e-mail forwarded to *my* e-mail account, but I don't want anyone to trace Dan Welch to me. I don't know how it works, but that's how they always find you on detective shows.

I couldn't sign in to Dan Welch's account. I forgot his password. I always think I should write down my passwords so I don't forget them, but what if I lose that piece of paper and someone finds it?

When Dan Welch got his e-mail account, I remember thinking he had a really good password. I think I thought that because no one would ever guess it. No one, including me.

There's something I use for a lot of my passwords, and even though I'm pretty sure I didn't use it for Dan Welch, I tried it. Wrong. I can't click "Forget your password?" because they'll send the password to Dan's e-mail, which I can't get into without his password.

I looked around my room, hoping to find a clue. Beach ball? Pillow? Detroit? We were getting ready to go to Detroit when I opened this account. I don't remember ever typing the word "Detroit," but I was so nervous opening Dan's e-mail account, I could have typed anything. I tried Detroit. Wrong. I hate when this happens.

Then I got a text from Buzz.

Wot u duin

He means "What are you doing?" Buzz actually can't spell in real life, but you don't notice it so much when he texts. I texted back.

Unpacking.

I tried to get back to work remembering the password, but it's hard to concentrate when someone's texting you. You're waiting for the next text. It could come in a few seconds or it could come in a minute or in ten minutes or never. It came in about a minute.

Play we

He's asking me if I want to play Wii baseball with him. He knows it's "Wii," not "we." It says Wii on the box, it says Wii on the controller, it says Wii when you play it, and he plays it every day.

If I was asking him the same thing, I would say "Play Wii?" Then he would know I was asking to come over and play Wii, not just telling him I was playing Wii. But I'm not Buzz. I texted back.

No can do.

That means I can't. It's something my dad says. I like the sound of it. I don't know if Buzz will understand, but since the word "no" is in there, he'll probably get the idea.

Buzz isn't his real name. His real name is Balthazar, but when he was little, his brother had trouble saying it, so everyone started calling him Buzz. Everyone except his mom. She was the one who picked Balthazar. His brother is Zephryn.

My computer screen turned off while I was texting with Buzz. When I moved the mouse it came on again, and when I saw the sign-on screen for Dan Welch's e-mail account, I knew his password right away. Now that I remember what it is, I can't believe I forgot it. It's such an obvious password. Unfortunately, I can't tell you why.

I typed in the password and hit ENTER and the account opened. There's one new e-mail. It's from her.

I'm scared to open it. I almost prayed, but I stopped just in time. I don't believe in praying for things like a meeting with a Vice President of Production. I think you can hope that things like that will happen, but I don't think it's right to get God involved.

I don't actually know if God listens to every

little prayer of every single person in the world. And who knows, maybe animals pray, too. Either way, that would be a lot of prayers. I'm sure some of them are for much bigger things than a meeting with someone at my trial run company. I don't want to distract God from the big stuff.

So instead of praying, I said out loud, "Whatever it is, it'll be okay."

To: Dan Welch Management
From: Stefanie V. President

Dear Dan,

Thirteen? Really? Sure, I'd love to meet Sean Rosen. Please call my office and set something up. My assistant's name is Brad. Good to hear from you.

Stefanie—555-123-4567 (not her real number)

I can't believe it. I read it six times. She wants to meet me. Thank you, Dan Welch.

chapter 16

I have three problems.

Problem 1: If someone, for example Stefanie's assistant Brad, talks on the phone with Dan Welch, and then talks to me, he's probably going to notice that we have the exact same voice.

I know the sound of my voice. When you do podcasts, especially if you edit them (most people don't, but they should), you know the sound of your voice. You may not *like* the sound of your voice, but you know it.

I practiced doing a different voice. A Dan Welch voice. What would he sound like? I tried a few different voices, and I realized that I can't really hear myself when I'm talking. I got my digital voice recorder, and I pretended I was Dan Welch calling Brad to set up a meeting for Sean.

I waited a little while, then I listened to it. Then I listened to one of my podcasts. My Dan Welch voice sounds exactly like my Sean Rosen voice. No. What it sounds like exactly is me trying not to sound like me. I know some people can do a lot of different voices. Unfortunately, I'm not one of those people. So if Brad only makes appointments for Stefanie V. President by phone, I'm in trouble.

Problem 2: Dan Welch told Stefanie I have an idea for a movie. Or a whole series of movies. At our meeting, she might possibly want to hear that idea.

The problem is, right now I have my big entertainment idea, which will affect TV, theater, games, and especially movies. But I don't have an idea for an actual movie. Or a series of movies.

I'm not sure why Dan Welch said I did, but I guess he knew what he was doing, because Stefanie would love to meet me.

It's not like I ever tried to come up with an idea

for a movie and couldn't do it. I just never tried. I've *seen* a lot of movies. I love movies. I guess I'll just think of a story for a movie that I would want to see, and maybe Stefanie will want to see it too.

The smart thing would be to get to work right away and try to come up with a great movie idea, no matter how long it takes. Then when I have one, Dan Welch can set up the meeting.

The problem is, I'm pretty busy right now. I have school, homework, my podcast, chores. I don't know how long it takes to think of a movie idea.

I do know that after I come up with one, even if I think it's great at first, pretty soon I'll start wondering if it's good enough. Then I'll try to come up with a better one. That could happen like forty times.

No. We'll make an appointment first and I'll work on the idea after. That way I'll know exactly how much time I have to come up with a movie. Or a series of movies.

Problem 3: Stefanie works in Los Angeles. I don't live anywhere near Los Angeles. To get from where I live to Los Angeles, most people fly.

I actually wouldn't mind driving. I like long car trips. Unfortunately, I won't have my license for another two years and five months.

My dad also likes long car trips. The problem is, if I suggest that we drive to Los Angeles and he has to miss work for a week, he's going to ask a lot of questions. Even if he doesn't, my mom definitely will. If she wasn't a nurse, she would be a detective.

I don't necessarily want to tell them about Dan Welch. They don't know the entertainment business. They might not understand.

It's not like I was sitting in my room and suddenly decided it would be fun to have an imaginary manager. I *had* to do it. I tried going to the company by myself. They accused me of stealing their ideas. They said I needed an agent or a manager. I tried to get an agent. I tried to get a manager.

I guess I could have just waited until Martin Manager decided he was ready to work with me. But who knows if that would ever happen. If it never did, that would be really, really sad.

think I solved one of my problems this morning. Skype. It's perfect. I was taking a shower when I thought of this. Stefanie V. President knows I'm thirteen. I go to school. Unfortunately, I can't just jump on a plane to have a meeting with her.

I was so happy I figured this out that I wanted to tell Dan Welch. When I remembered that I can't, it made me feel lonely. If anyone could understand all this, it's him, and I can't call him.

When I think about him, he's a real person. I can't tell you what he looks like. I don't know how tall he is or how old he is or what color hair he has. But he feels like an actual grown-up who wants to help me with my career.

I can't be Dan Welch on the phone, but I think I know who can. Ethan. I've only heard him say one word so far, but trust me, he doesn't sound anything like a kid. And he won't blab to anyone about my imaginary manager because he never talks. It's perfect.

I wrote a little Dan Welch script for Ethan, then after school I followed him. He was by himself, as usual. "Hey, Ethan." He didn't turn around. He might not have heard me. He's so much bigger than me that his ears are a long distance from my mouth.

I started walking next to him. "Hi, Ethan. I'm Sean."

"I know." He knew because Mr. Knapp called on me in history this morning, and it turned into a whole big thing. Ethan kept walking. I had to hurry to keep up.

"What are you doing right now?"

"Walking."

"Right. I have a project I can use a little help with. Not sports. At my house."

"Something on a high shelf?"

"Funny. No. Trust me, Ethan. This will be really fun."

"It will?"

"I'm pretty sure it will." Listening to him talk, I know this is going to work.

He came over. We had some pretzels and Cokes in the kitchen. My parents were both at work. I brought my laptop and the script down from my bedroom.

"Let's do this in the dining room. It's the most like an office. Why don't you sit . . . there." Ethan sat down. I handed him a piece of paper. "Okay, all you have to do is read these lines. One at a time, in order. When I point to you."

"Right now?"

"Yes. We're going to rehearse the whole thing before we actually make the call. Ready? Just the first line." I pointed at him.

ETHAN: **Is this Brad?**

"Very good. Then Brad says yes. Then you say the next line." I pointed at him again.

ETHAN: This is Dan Welch. Stefanie asked me to call you about setting up a meeting with my client Sean Rosen.

"Excellent. Then Brad will say something. Then you say the next line."

ETHAN: Sean can't make it to Los Angeles. How would Stefanie feel about having the meeting on Skype?

"Okay, but remember to wait until I point. The timing has to be exactly right."

"Sorry."

"No, Ethan . . . it's totally fine. You're doing great. Okay, I'll be sitting right here, listening on another phone. Depending what Brad says next, I'll type out your next line and you'll read it right off my computer screen."

"Okay."

"Good. Now let's really rehearse it."

"What do you mean?"

"This time, sound like you're actually talking to someone on the phone. Wait! I know. Here's my phone. I'll go back into the kitchen. When you're ready, hit the green button. You'll be calling the house phone. When I answer, I'll be Brad and you'll be Dan Welch."

"Okay."

I went into the kitchen. The phone rang. I answered. "Stefanie President's office."

ETHAN: **Is this Brad?**

"Yes. Who's this?"

ETHAN: **This is Dan Welch. Stefanie asked me to call you about setting up a meeting with my client Sean Rosen.**

"Ethan . . . we're just going to stop for a second. Can you try that last line again? It still sounds like you're reading it. Which you are, I know. But can you try to make it sound like you're actually talking to someone? Like in real life?"

"I can try."

He tried. After a few minutes, I figured out why it wasn't working. When Ethan talks in real life, he sounds exactly like he's reading. And not reading with expression. I came back into the dining room to work with him.

It was actually funny. I would read a line the way I thought it should sound, then Ethan would try to imitate me, and he would always sound exactly like himself. Then we would both crack up. It was never going to work. We ended up watching a couple of my podcasts instead. I think he liked them.

Ethan never asked me who Dan Welch is or who Stefanie President is or anything. And even though it didn't work, I was right. It was fun.

chapter 18

Since Ethan can't be Dan Welch on the phone, I'm going to pretend I'm Dan Welch's assistant and call Brad myself. All I need to get from Brad is his e-mail address. Then Dan can e-mail him and set up my meeting.

I wonder if Brad always answers Stefanie V. President's phone. I would hate to call and actually get *her*. I guess if she answers, I can just hang up. But I hate hanging up on people. Or when someone hangs up on me.

It'll be okay. None of the people in show business I called so far answered their own phone. Brad probably always answers unless he's at lunch, and I think lunchtime in Los Angeles is over.

What if he asks who I am and why I want his e-mail address? I'll just say I'm Dan Welch's assistant, and Dan wants to set up a meeting with Stefanie for someone he manages.

What if he asks me my name? I can't be Sean Rosen. I should be ready with something else. Chris. That's a name I always wanted to have. I don't mind Sean, except when you have a name that doesn't sound like it looks, you have to spell it all the time. It's actually kind of annoying.

Chris might be like that, too. You don't pronounce the *H*, and there are different ways to spell it. But I like it. And when Brad hears my voice on the phone, if he thinks I'm a girl, it's okay because there are girls named Chris. I actually don't think I sound like a girl.

I got my phone. First I blocked Caller ID. I learned this from my dad, who sometimes does it when he calls people who didn't pay their plumbing bill. Then I called Stefanie's number.

VOICE: Stefanie President's office.
ME: Oh, hi. Is this Brad?

BRAD:	Yes. Who's this?
ME:	Oh, this is Chris from Dan Welch Management.

I was glad I had a name ready.

BRAD:	Hi, Chris.
ME:	Hi, Brad. We wanted to get your e-mail address.
BRAD:	Oh, sure. It's brad._____@ _____.com
ME:	Thanks.
BRAD:	Sure. What is this for? A screening, I hope.
ME:	Actually . . . I'm not really sure.

Actually, I forgot what I was planning to say because I was thinking *I'd* like to go to a screening, too.

BRAD:	Okay. I guess I'll find out.
ME:	I guess so.

That was easy. Brad sounds like a nice guy. I hope he's not mad when he finds out that we're not inviting him to a screening. Maybe I should have told him that it isn't a screening, so he doesn't get his hopes up. But Brad doesn't sound like the kind of guy who would want revenge. If we *were* having a screening, I would invite him. Actually, when the movie I still don't have an idea for has a screening, I'll make sure Brad is invited.

To: Brad
From: Dan Welch Management

Dear Brad,

I manage Sean Rosen. Stefanie asked me to contact you to set up a meeting for Sean to talk to her about his movie idea. Unfortunately, Sean has commitments that will keep him away from L.A., so I'm wondering if they can have this meeting on Skype.

The best time for Sean is after 2 pm L.A. time. This week

is kind of full for him, so if we can schedule the meeting for next week or the week after, that would be better.

I'm excited for Stefanie and Sean to meet. He's a unique guy, and this is a cool idea that no one else has heard yet.

Thanks, Brad.
Best,
Dan

I read it over about fifteen times. I like the way Dan Welch writes. I'm pretty sure that people in Los Angeles call it "L.A." Dan wasn't kidding when he said that no one has heard this idea yet. No one including me.

I read it again, then I finally hit SEND. Then I shivered. Not because I'm cold, but because I still can't believe any of this is happening.

Because that's what it feels like. Something that's happening to me, not something I'm actually doing. I know that might be hard to explain to the FBI.

Dan told Brad I'm going to be busy this week, which is true. Besides my podcast, this is the week we take everyone's picture for the e-yearbook.

My school used to have a paper yearbook. Well, it used to have no yearbook, then for years it had a paper yearbook. Then last year the school ran out of money and had to fire six teachers. So now we have an e-yearbook, which isn't bad except you can't write in it the way people used to write in each other's yearbooks.

Our e-yearbook has an Autograph Wall that you can "write" on, but it's not the same. I love reading what people wrote in my parents' high school yearbooks. This one is from my dad's.

Jackie, you dog—

Never forget that night at Gino's or those nights after bowling or . . . Damn! I forget.

Stay cool, you fool.

Tremor

That's right. Tremor. Not Trevor. It was a nickname. His real name is Roger. My dad won't tell me the story of Roger's nickname. Dad calls him Trem. We ran into him once in a store. I was a little surprised my dad was ever friends with him, but they were in high school a long time ago, and those nights Tremor wrote about in the yearbook were in ninth grade.

Here's one from my mom's yearbook.

Dearest Elise,

If we're lucky, we have one special friend in our life. Someone whose shoulder we can cry on. Someone who can always make us laugh. For me, that friend is you. I'm very lucky.

Loads of love,

Dawn

My mom read that and thought it was the most beautiful thing anyone ever said to her. Until she read her cousin Angela's yearbook. Dawn wrote the exact same thing to her. Word for word. Most people didn't know that Angela and Mom were cousins. Dawn, for example. That would never happen on the Autograph Wall.

One of my jobs on the yearbook is to check people in when they come to get their picture taken. I like it because I sort of get to know everyone in the school. After I check them in, I make sure their picture actually gets taken. Then I put an X next to their name on the list.

I check the pictures because every once in a while, the photographer, who's just a kid in my school, thinks he took a picture of someone, but he didn't. Or sometimes it's just a really bad picture. Like someone's eyes are closed or something like that. When that happens, I suggest taking another picture. That's not part of my job, but who wants to have a bad picture in the yearbook?

In last year's yearbook, there was a really bad picture of someone, like embarrassingly bad. It was a kid who once said something really mean to me. It was in sixth grade. He said it in front of other kids, and the thing he said got to be a little famous. He and I used to be friends, but not after that. Actually, it's the same kid whose dad built the tree house. Doug.

I knew I should have told the photographer to

take another picture of Doug, but I didn't. Doug probably doesn't know I could have saved him from having a bad picture in the yearbook, but *I* know. It's not something I feel good about. Maybe I won't be in the Publication Room tomorrow when Doug comes in for his picture.

Mr. Hollander came in at the beginning of today's picture session. This was my first time seeing him since Dan Welch became my manager. It was a little weird, because Dan Welch sounds a lot like Mr. Hollander. I wanted to tell Mr. Hollander about Dan Welch, but I decided not to. If I get arrested, I don't want anyone else to get in trouble.

got home and opened Dan Welch's e-mail account. There was something there. I was excited that Brad wrote back so quickly. Except he didn't.

To: Dan Welch Management
From: Dan Welch

Hey, Dan Welch!

It's me, Dan Welch. No, your not looking in the mirror. I'm another guy named Dan Welch. How do you like having our name? I like it fine. I've had it for 44 years now.

I came across you today when I was googling myself. You ever do that? I'm kinda addicted to it. Its mostly my ebay stuff that comes up, but there's a whole bunch of other Dan Welches out there. This was the first time I saw you.

Hey, your guy Sean is pretty good. I watched every one of his podcasts. Im not sure what there is to manage about podcasts, but knock em dead, buddy.

I'm in business 6 years now. Collectibles. You name it, I got it. Check out my website. UNameItIGotIt.com Are you a collector? I got everything. Sports, beany babies, franklin mint, hummels, unicorns, barbys, everything. TEll me what your looking for and I'll get it for you.

Who else do you manage besides Sean? I wonder if I need a manager. Seriously, if you ever want to work on something together or just kick around some ideas, give me a jingle. My number is 555-888-5555 (not his real number).

Okay buddy,
Dan

P.S. What's your middle name? Mine is Kelvin. I know. By the way, I have a certified strand of Chester Alan Arthur's hair. He used to be president. In case you need an unusual present for someone.

Wow. Even though I got the name from yogurt and grape juice, I guess there are some actual people named Dan Welch. I don't think Stefanie or Brad or anyone in the entertainment business will mix up my Dan Welch with this Dan Welch.

It feels a little weird that Collectibles Dan Welch went on my website and watched all of my podcasts. I know they're just sitting there on the internet for anyone to watch, and I actually *want* people to watch them. But I didn't know if anyone who doesn't already know me ever would.

I know the whole idea of being in the

entertainment business is making movies and TV shows and music and games for millions of people I don't already know. It's just strange to read an e-mail from one of them. I'm glad Collectibles Dan Welch likes the podcasts. I guess he does if he watched all of them. I'm not going to write back. Anyway, he wrote to Dan Welch, not to me.

I actually have to get to work on my podcast. This is how I put one together: I go to a place in my town. It could be any kind of place—a store, a park, a gas station. I interview people who work there and other people who are there that day shopping or walking their dog or getting gas. I also take pictures.

It's usually a Saturday or Sunday afternoon. I stay for about two hours and I usually interview about eight people. I try to use every person I interview in the podcast. I would feel bad if I interviewed someone and they were waiting and waiting for the podcast to be uploaded, then they listened to it and they weren't even on it.

The questions I ask in the interviews are a

little bit about the place and a little bit about the person I'm talking to. I also record all the different sounds of the place. My digital voice recorder is small, but it has two very good microphones built in.

Then I write a song that feels like it goes with the place. I edit everything, I upload it, and that's my podcast. Each piece is short, so it's very convenient. You can watch one piece or every piece on your phone or computer or whatever.

The bar mitzvah podcast will be different. Besides being in Detroit, it's going to be in two parts so I can fit in all the places and people. Sometimes it's hard to find people who want to be interviewed. Not at this bar mitzvah. When people saw me recording someone, they came over and said, "Me next. Interview me next." I'm talking about adults, not kids.

This was a very noisy bar mitzvah. The loud music made everyone shout, and sometimes it's hard to hear the questions and answers. I tried every filter and noise reduction thing on my computer, but I just can't use some of the inter-views. Like the one I did with my grandmother.

I came downstairs to ask my parents what to do about Grandma. "Forget it, Seany. I ain't touching that with a fork."

Then my mom said, "Before you put it online, send her an e-mail and tell her why she isn't in it. Do it tonight."

"Mom . . . can you do it?" They both laughed.

To: Thorny Rosen
From: Sean Rosen

Dear Grandma,

How are you?

It was great to see you in Detroit.

Remember our interview at the bar mitzvah party?

Remember how noisy that party was? Even though you were talking loud, I can't use your interview in my podcast. There was too much noise. You'll still be in some other parts of the podcast.

I know you're disappointed and if you want to skip my birthday present this year, you can.

Love,

Sean

chapter 20

I can't stop staring at my computer. Is Brad ever going to write back to Dan Welch? I thought it would be really fast. Like he'd get the e-mail and call out to Stefanie, "Dan Welch wants to know if you can have your meeting with Sean Rosen on Skype." She'd say, "Sure. Why not?" He'd say, "Good. I'll take care of it." Then she'd say, "Thanks, Brad. You're the best."

Now I'm starting to get worried. Maybe *this* is what happened.

BRAD: Dan Welch wants to know...
STEFANIE: Dan <u>who</u>?

BRAD: Dan Welch. From Dan Welch
           Management. It's about your
           meeting with Sean Rosen.

STEFANIE: Sean who?

BRAD: Sean Rosen. His client. Dan
           said you wanted to meet him.

STEFANIE: I did? Why? Who is he? What
           does he do?

BRAD: I have no idea, but whoever
           he is, he wants to have the
           meeting on Skype.

STEFANIE: Why? Is he shooting a movie
           in Africa?

Maybe Brad is on vacation. Maybe Stefanie is on vacation. Maybe she has chicken pox. If she does, she'll want to meet on Skype, because she can't go to the office. No, she won't. She won't want anyone to see her with chicken pox.

It's only been a day since Dan sent the e-mail, but it was a long day. French was awful. She's never going to call on me again. Then I forgot to be away from the Publication Room when Doug came to have his picture taken.

I tried to act really busy with my list, but he came over to where I was sitting. I didn't know what he was going to do. He bent down, and right in my ear, so only I could hear, said, "Thanks for last year's picture, you little _____."

I'm not actually little, but I guess compared to Doug I am. I would tell you what he called me, but I don't use words like that.

It was creepy. Like he might show up in a bad dream tonight.

Why am I still sitting here staring at Dan Welch's empty inbox, not working on my home-work, not working on my podcast, not playing Ricochet Roulette? Fortunately, I got a text from Brianna.

Call me right now.

Brianna doesn't know about Dan Welch or my whole show-business career. No one does. Well, Ethan knows a tiny bit, but he'll never tell anyone. Not everyone can keep secrets. My mom can. She doesn't like to lie, but she can definitely keep her mouth shut. My dad can't keep a secret.

You tell him it's a secret, and twenty minutes later he tells someone. Not to be mean. It's like he doesn't believe in secrets. I learned this the hard way.

It's weird to be in the middle of something so important and not tell any of the people I see every day. Well, I guess it's not that weird for me. I've always had a lot of private things. I think that happens more when you don't have brothers and sisters.

Brianna (two brothers) is the opposite of private. At first I thought she was telling me all those personal things because I was such a good friend and she could trust me. Then I found out she tells a lot of people.

That's one of the reasons I don't tell her much. But even if I wanted to, it would be hard to do. Brianna doesn't stop talking long enough. I don't mind. It's like reading a book where you never have to turn the pages. She just keeps going until you have to leave.

Today Brianna was talking about plastic surgery. Her mom had it yesterday. Brianna says she's addicted to it. I've known her mom for a few years, and she definitely looks different now, but it's hard to say if it's better or worse. I have no idea which parts are plastic.

Brianna said her parents aren't talking to each other again. I wonder why they always fight. Brianna thinks it's because they didn't used to have money and now they do. I don't know what that has to do with it. I'm lucky my parents like each other.

She asked me what I think of her new profile picture on Facebook. She changes it every few days. I haven't been on Facebook for a little while, and I was just about to go there when a new e-mail popped into Dan Welch's inbox. I have to get off the phone.

I quickly muted the sound on my computer and called myself from Skype. "Brianna, can you hold on a sec? I have another call." I switched to the other call, and for some reason I had a little fake conversation with myself out loud. I guess part of me believes that if you're on the phone with some-one and you put them on hold, they can hear your other conversation. I don't actually know if that's true.

When I got back on with Brianna, I said, "Did you hear that?" She said no. I said it was my mom calling from downstairs reminding me that I promised to help her in the yard. I felt bad lying, but I can't keep talking about Facebook when something important is happening.

I said good-bye and opened the e-mail.

To: Dan Welch Management
From: Brad

Dear Dan,

Stefanie would be happy to have a meeting with Sean on Skype. In fact, she loves that idea. You said you wanted to do it after this week. I'm not sure if you knew, but Stefanie goes on maternity leave next week, so she'd like to do it tomorrow afternoon at five our time. I hope that works for you.

She's very excited about hearing Sean's idea. We all are.

It will be Stefanie, our three Directors of Development, and me. Dan, will you be there with Sean? We're looking forward to meeting you both. Our Skype address is

_____.

Please confirm. See you tomorrow.

Cheers,
Brad

What?! Tomorrow?!! Dan . . . Why didn't we wait until I actually had an idea?

I guess it's good that we didn't, because Stefanie would already be on maternity leave. But I was sure I'd have more time than this. Like a weekend at least.

So in the next twenty-six hours, I have to do my homework, go to school, finish my podcast and upload it, come up with a movie idea that could possibly be a whole series of movies, and figure out how to explain it to five people at one of the biggest entertainment companies in the world. And find someone who can be Dan Welch at the Skype meeting.

I suddenly got very, very tired. It was 4:37 in the afternoon, but all I wanted to do was go to bed. It doesn't make sense that when you have more to do than you ever have in your whole life that you would go to bed, but I know I won't get anything done unless I get some sleep.

Unfortunately, when you're worried about things, even if you're really, really tired, it's hard to fall asleep. You keep thinking about the things you're worried about. You just hear them over and over in your head.

Here's what I do when that happens. I listen to a podcast. Not one of my own, because then I would think about how it could be better. Then I'd have to add "Fix the podcast" to my list of things to do when I'm not so tired. Instead, I listen to someone else's podcast.

There's a million of them on the internet. I try to find one that's sort of interesting, so I'll actually want to listen to it, but not too interesting because then I'll try to stay awake and listen to the whole thing. It actually works. I usually use science podcasts, because I'm sort of interested in science, but not too interested. Today was "Appalachian Coal Mining."

I know everyone is different with sleep, but for me, if I fall asleep for even fifteen minutes, I feel much, much better when I wake up. It worked today. I woke up, I read Brad's e-mail again, and now, instead of being scared, I'm excited.

A vice president of a huge company wants to hear my movie idea. A few weeks ago this same company accused me of stealing *their* ideas. Now, thanks to Dan Welch, they're willing to talk to me. And I don't have to figure out how to get to Los Angeles. Stefanie actually loves my idea of doing it on Skype. This is all very, very good.

At least I *think* it is. I wonder if I should be concentrating on my big idea and the company I actually want to work with on it. What if someone else comes up with my same big idea? What if what I'm really good at is big ideas, not movies?

This might sound conceited, but I actually think I'm going to be good at both. But even if I'm not good at movies, I won't be wasting much time on them. My meeting is tomorrow.

And I'm not sure exactly how, but I have a feeling we're going to learn things from this trial run that will make it easier for Dan Welch and me to sell my big idea.

Good. Let's get to work. When I have a lot to do, I make a list. I got that from my mom. She loves lists. I once saw one of her lists where one of the things on the list was "Make a list." Here's mine.

1. Have Dan Welch confirm the Skype meeting.
2. Have Dan tell Brad he won't be at the Skype meeting.
3. Go to www.SeanRosen.com and post an announcement explaining why the new podcast isn't ready.
4. Do enough homework to get through school tomorrow.
5. Come up with an idea for a movie or a whole series of movies.

chapter 21

To: Brad
From: Dan Welch Management

Dear Brad,

Tomorrow at five your time is perfect for Sean. Sorry I won't be able to join you, but I'm sure I'll get a full report.

Best, Dan

• • •

Attention podcast friends:

I know it's been a little while since my last podcast.

I'm putting together a very special two-part podcast. Part one will be ready soon, I promise.

We've been getting some excellent comments from listeners.

> (Okay. One comment from one listener—
> Collectibles Dan Welch)

This week I suggest you look at the podcasts on the site, and if you missed one, now is the perfect time to catch up. If you never missed one, maybe there's one you want to see again.

See you soon.

Best, Sean

Okay, I took care of number 1, number 2, and number 3 on my list. I spent a half hour doing homework. I'm so lucky that math is easy for me.

The only thing I have left to do is number 5. The movie idea. I love movies. How hard can it be to come up with one?

It's not like I actually have to *make* a movie by tomorrow. Or even write a script for a movie by tomorrow. All I need for tomorrow is an idea for a movie. Or a series of movies.

Maybe a bike ride would be a good way to empty out my mind. I know I don't have much time, but I like this time of day. It's still light out, but there are all these cool shadows. I rode to the firehouse and back, which is only like ten minutes, but that was enough. I feel good. I'm ready to get to work.

I wonder what would be a better way to do this— think about one movie or think about a series of movies. What are some of the big series of movies? Toy Story, Shrek, Harry Potter, Lord of the Rings, Pirates of the Caribbean. I looked online. The Toy Storys made almost 2 billion dollars, the Pirates of the Caribbeans made more than 2.6 billion, and the Shreks made about 3 billion.

When I think about coming up with an idea that will make even 1 billion dollars I want to go back to sleep. So for now, I'm just going to think about an idea for one movie.

Okay. A movie. What's the movie about? It's about a kid. A kid my age. A kid my age who comes up with an incredible invention. What does the invention do? It makes his school disappear.

What would happen if my school disappeared? My parents would find another school for me to go to. What if the new school is worse than my own school? This movie is getting depressing. I'm going to start over.

Okay, it's a movie about a kid like me. Why should it be about a kid like me? Would I want to see a movie about myself? Maybe not. But maybe. It would depend on what actor was playing me. Oh no. Now I'm thinking about what actor should play me in a movie, and I don't even have an idea for a movie.

Maybe the kid doesn't have to be just like me. Okay, it's not me. It's a guy named . . . Chris. He's older than me. He's fifteen. And he has a younger sister. Her name is Chloe. Just in case you don't know that name, the *Ch* at the beginning sounds like a *K*, and the *e* at the end gets pronounced, and it's an *e* like in the word *be*.

I know this because a few years ago I was reading out loud in class, and whatever I was reading had the name Chloe. I tried to figure out how to say it, but I couldn't, so I just stopped reading. My teacher tried to get me to guess, but I wouldn't. I had no idea how you would ever say that name.

Okay. Chris and Chloe. Would parents actually name their kids that? Yes. I know some twins named Willy and Lily. I guess their real names are actually William and Liliana, but everyone calls them Willy and Lily.

Okay. Chris is fifteen and Chloe is twelve. He looks out for her in that older brother way. I guess. I never actually had an older brother and I never actually *was* someone's older brother, but that's how I picture it.

Their parents are crazy busy. They both have big jobs and they both earn lots of money. They're both on their iPhones all the time. Really. All the time. Then they come home and they keep

working, plus they're involved in all of Chris's and Chloe's activities.

Chris is a tennis player and Chloe is a gymnast. Neither of them is like a superstar athlete, but they're both into it. On weekends one parent goes to a tennis match with Chris and the other goes to a gymnastics meet with Chloe. The parents each take turns being with each kid because they think that's the right thing to do. But whether they're at gymnastics with Chloe or tennis with Chris, the parents sometimes miss things, because they're always on their iPhones.

Chris and Chloe are also very busy, with school and homework and activities, plus hours and hours of tennis and gymnastics. They all really need a vacation.

That's how far I got when my mom called me to come eat dinner. Not on my phone, like I pretended to Brianna. My mom just yells. I have to stop working, but I got a good start. I'm not so worried about my meeting now. I'm excited to see what's going to happen to Chris and Chloe. I always like vacation movies.

chapter 22

It turned out that stopping for dinner was a very good thing. Partly because we had mashed potatoes, but mostly because my parents gave me an idea for my vacation movie. It was a terrible idea in real life, but perfect for my movie.

We were eating dinner, and first my mom told us about a patient she had. She's not allowed to say their names, but it's okay to talk about them. Then my dad complained about the six-person hot tub he just installed. I don't get why anyone would ever take a bath, so to me, taking one with five other people is only a little bit weirder.

Then I said to my parents, "Name your favorite vacation." My dad said Disney World. He likes rides. My mom said New York. She likes taking the subway and trying new kinds of food.

I was still deciding about mine when my dad said, "Seany, what do you think about your mom and me having a little second honeymoon?" I heard about their first honeymoon. It was kind of a mess. They didn't have much money and their families didn't exactly want them to get married.

They drove to Niagara Falls in an old car that broke down on the way. The only place they could afford to stay was a YMCA where men and women were on separate floors. They each had a roommate they never met before.

So a second honeymoon sounded like a good idea. I asked where we were going, and they just looked at each other. Then I remembered that a honeymoon means no kids. I said, "Just kidding," but we all knew I wasn't. Then I said, "Seriously, where are you planning to go?"

They didn't know. Before they decided, they wanted to see how I felt about them going on a vacation without me. I felt fine. Mostly. I guess it depends where they go. Then my mom said,

"Maybe you can stay with Grandma." She meant my dad's mom (Thorny Rosen). We call the other one Mary Lou.

No! No way! It's bad enough you're going away without me. Don't make me stay with her. I don't like her condo. I don't like her friends. I don't know how long you're going for, but it's too long to leave me alone with her.

I didn't actually say those things, but from the look on my face, I was pretty sure they got it. Then my mom said, "Or she could stay here."

No! That's even worse! Whenever she stays with us, she breaks something—the TV, the dishwasher, the computer. Once she actually broke the back door. She changes things all over the house. And she always wants to talk. And when you talk to her, she asks you all these big questions. For an afternoon, yes. But a whole week? No!

I didn't actually say any of that, either. What I actually said was, "I'm not a child. I can stay by myself." I knew they wouldn't let me. My dad remembers how he was when he was thirteen. I wouldn't leave that kid alone in a house either.

"I can stay with Aunt Gigi and Uncle Dave." Everyone knew that was a good idea. My cousins are away at college, and Gigi and Dave are lonely. I really like them and they really like me. That was the end of the discussion.

After dinner I went upstairs to get back to work on my movie idea. Now I know exactly what to do. When the movie starts, Chris and Chloe's parents tell them, "For the first time since you two were born, we're going on a vacation by ourselves. Kind of a second honeymoon. And to be sure it's actually a vacation, we're going to a place where there's no cell phone or internet service. It's in the wilderness in Bolivia. It looks beautiful."

Chris is excited. He thinks this means that he and Chloe will have the house to themselves.

"Actually, no. You and Chloe are going to spend the week with Grandpa and Grandma."

The kids are not happy. "They don't have Wi-Fi." "They don't even have cable." "They eat weird food." "Grandma hugs too hard."

Then their mom says, "Well, here's what they say about *you*. 'They have the attention span of an amoeba.' 'All they do is stare at screens and shoot things.' 'Every time they're in a bad mood they have to tell all four thousand of their "friends."'" Ouch.

Then their dad says, "We already bought our tickets to Bolivia. You'll survive. It's only a week. I had to live with them for eighteen years."

The name of the movie is *A Week with Your Grandparents*.

Their mom and dad go to Bolivia, and Chris and Chloe go to their grandparents' house. It's an old house, not like a haunted house, but one of those houses that was built when people were smaller. Chris and Chloe each hate something about their room. The first meal is some kind of brown stew with rice. No one knows what to talk about at dinner.

Then we see the parents. They're in Bolivia, also having dinner, outside in the wilderness. No one there speaks English. They don't know what to talk about at dinner either. Every once in a while, when one of them isn't looking, the other one checks their iPhone, but there's really no service there.

Back at the house, Grandpa starts to tell one of his stories. "When I was your age . . ." Chloe can't help it. She knows it's going to be boring, so under the table she checks her phone. Grandpa sees it and he stops talking. He gets up and leaves the table. Chloe doesn't even notice. She's chatting with a friend.

Grandma gets mad. "Hey! Hey! What's wrong with you? I know you think we're old and annoying, but come on. We're sitting at a table together. It's only you and us. When we talk to you and you don't even look up, it hurts our feelings."

Chris and Chloe feel bad. Grandma tells them there's a lot they don't know about their family. "You know that Grandpa is a biochemist, right?" They probably heard that before and they say yes, but they don't completely know what a biochemist does. "Well, he's a great one, and he's an amazing inventor, too. He deserves a little respect."

Chloe goes and apologizes to Grandpa, and the kids get him to talk about his inventions. The best invention, according to him, is something Grandma won't let him sell. They tried it out and it works. Grandma was sure this invention would be super popular, but she was afraid it might be bad for the world, so that was the end of it.

Grandpa explains the invention. It's a virtual reality time machine. It makes you feel like you're in a room with a person you actually know, but at an earlier time in their life. You choose the date you want to go back to. You stay your same age, but you can see the way they were on the exact date you choose. You actually feel like you're in the same room with them. You can talk to them. You can smell and taste things in the room and you can even touch things. It's all virtual.

"No way." That was Chloe. Chris doesn't say anything, but he looks like he doesn't believe it either.

"In all modesty . . . ," Grandpa says, "it's so convincing that it's impossible to imagine if you haven't experienced it."

Chris finally says something. "Grandpa . . . please???"

Grandpa looks happy Chris wants to try it, but Grandma says no.

Chloe says, "We're not afraid. We're braver than you."

Grandma wants to call Chris and Chloe's parents to ask them if it's okay, but they can't be reached. We see them in Bolivia in their tent. They can't figure out how to open the high-tech sleeping bags they bought for the trip. It's very, very dark. They're trying to read the instructions using the light from their iPhones, but the batteries are dying.

Grandma knows how much it would mean to Grandpa to show his invention to Chris and Chloe. He wants his grandchildren to be proud of him.

Grandma puts one hand on Chloe's shoulder and the other on Chris's. She looks right at them. "On one condition. But it's a real condition. You can't *ever* tell *anyone*. Think about this, because believe me . . . you're gonna want to. But you can't. Ever. Can you swear to me that you'll keep this a secret?"

Chris and Chloe don't exactly understand what this thing is and they don't actually believe it works, but there's no way they're not going to try it, so they swear. Grandpa flips a coin and Chloe wins. She's first. She wants to meet Grandpa when he was seventeen, the same age as this TV star she likes. She picks July 15, 1950.

They all go to the basement. Grandpa unlocks a door and takes them into his laboratory, a room they've never seen before. It's like a work room, not some mad scientist place with bubbling chemicals.

Grandpa takes out a glass slide and spits on it. He's giving the machine a sample of his DNA. He explains that our DNA has a memory of every single day of our lives. Then he takes everyone over to a chair next to a big metal box.

He says that when the machine starts working, everything will look and feel to Chloe like it's 1950, the year he was seventeen. She'll be exactly the same person she is now, but she'll be somewhere Grandpa actually was on July 15, 1950. His DNA will remember the place. It will feel like he's there with her, but he won't know who she is, because in 1950 he doesn't have any children or grandchildren yet. He's only seventeen.

Chloe sits in the chair and Grandpa opens the

metal box and puts her inside. Chloe is completely covered from the top of her head to her waist. Grandpa talks to her by pushing the button on the side of the machine that says TALK. It's right next to the button that says LISTEN. He adjusts the machine so she's comfortable.

Grandma pushes TALK. "Chloe, you don't have to do this." Then she pushes LISTEN.

"Forget it, Grandma. I'm doing it."

Grandpa pushes TALK. "Are you ready?" He pushes LISTEN.

"Beyond ready."

Grandpa pushes START. The machine lights up. There is the sound of a ticking clock. It keeps getting faster. One by one, five green lights come on. The names on the green lights are Sight, Sounds, Smell, Taste, and Touch. When all five lights are on, a little bell rings, and Chloe enters virtual reality. It's quiet for a few seconds, then from outside the machine, you can tell that Chloe is talking to someone, but you can't hear what they're saying. Then the movie switches to Chloe's virtual reality experience.

She's sitting on a stool at a soda fountain at a candy store the way candy stores looked in 1950. Grandpa is behind the counter. He works there. He's seventeen, and he doesn't look like a TV star, but he's a cool-looking kid. He's busy with other customers.

Chloe smells something. She looks over at a bunch of hot dogs rolling around on one of those old hot-dog cookers. Grandpa comes over. Chloe orders a hot dog and a Coke. Grandpa is really nice to her, but not in a flirting kind of way. She's still only twelve.

You can tell she thinks he's a super nice guy and cute, too. He explains the chemistry of how the soda fountain makes her Coke. Chloe isn't usually interested in science, but she listens really hard because she likes him and he knows how to explain things.

Grandma and Chris and Grandpa are in the basement watching Chloe in the machine. From the outside you can't tell what's going on. After a little while, Grandma hits the big red button that stops the machine. Then she pushes TALK. "Chloe . . .

Jeff Baron

are you okay?" Then she pushes LISTEN.

"Why did you stop it? I wanna go back!"

Grandpa looks at Grandma, who shakes her head. Grandpa helps Chloe out of the machine.

"Oh my God. Grandpa. Oh my God."

Grandma says to Grandpa, "See? We shouldn't have."

"Yes, you should. It was amazing. Grandpa, I love that candy store. Chris, you should have seen Grandpa. He was so cool. Not that you're not cool now, but . . . Oh my God!"

Grandma says, "Chloe . . . I just want to be sure you understand. *Nothing* happened. That was only what Grandpa *would* have said and *would* have done if you met him more than sixty years ago. But you didn't."

"Yes, I did."

Grandpa finally says something. To Grandma. "It *is* only virtual reality, but I wouldn't say it's 'nothing.'"

Chris is dying to try it, and like most grandparents, they want to be fair, so this time Grandma spits on the glass slide and Chris climbs into the machine. He wants to meet Grandma when she was his age, fifteen. He picks November 13, 1951.

We see Chris's virtual reality experience. He's in an old-fashioned high school where the guys are wearing ties and the girls are wearing dresses. Chris walks down the hall checking out how strange it all looks. He comes to a girl sitting at a table with a big sign. It says THANKSGIVING FUND. Everyone just walks past the girl at the table and Chris is about to also, when the girl says, "Get over here."

Chris looks around to see who she's talking to.

"You. Get over here."

He realizes the girl is Grandma. He nervously walks over to her.

"What are you having for Thanksgiving this year?"

Chris says, "What do you mean?"

"For dinner. For Thanksgiving dinner. What does your family eat?"

"Oh . . . turkey, stuffing, cranberry sauce . . . you know, the usual."

"Usual for you, but there are families right here

in this town that can't afford those things. Do you know how lucky you are?"

"I guess."

"You *guess*? Don't you think everyone should be able to have a nice Thanksgiving with their family?"

"Yeah."

"Well, what are you waiting for?"

This girl doesn't look or act like the other girls Chris sees in the school. Or like any girl Chris knows in real life. He ends up giving her all the money he has.

Suddenly, it's over. Grandma pushed the red button. Grandpa gets Chris out of the machine. He can't really talk. He just keeps staring at Grandma. Chloe wants to know what happened, but the only thing he'll say is it was something about high school.

Chris is freaked out. He has a big crush on his grandmother. He doesn't know what to do. She doesn't look like that fifteen-year-old girl now, but he can see that she's the same person. He always thought she was kind of bossy and annoying as a grandmother, and now he doesn't know what to think.

Chris says he's tired and goes upstairs. He calls his friend Zahid. Chris really wants to tell Zahid about Grandpa's invention, but since he swore he wouldn't, he can't.

Chloe comes to Chris's room. Neither of them believes what just happened. They swore not to tell anyone else, but they have to talk about it with each other. They're brother and sister, but they're also friends.

Now that they know Grandpa's virtual reality time machine actually works, Chris and Chloe think of other things they want to do with it. Chloe is having a fight with her friend April. April had a spa sleepover, and after their manicures, when April's mom took the girls to a restaurant for dinner, Taylor Swift was there and they all got her autograph. Of course Chloe heard about it and her feelings were hurt that she wasn't invited. April swears she texted Chloe about it the week before, but Chloe knows she never got that text.

If she can get some of April's DNA, Chloe can

go back to the Friday in school before the sleepover and find out the truth. Will April talk to Chloe about it or try to avoid her?

All Chris really wants to do is to spend more time with his grandmother when she was fifteen, but he's embarrassed about that. There's another reason he wants to go to the past. Chris is on his high school's varsity tennis team, which is pretty good for a sophomore. He always plays doubles, but Chris is sure he could win if he got to play singles.

Last week he had the perfect chance to ask the coach, but he got scared and didn't do it. He's been mad at himself ever since. If Chris can get some of the coach's DNA, he can use Grandpa's invention to go back to that day last week and talk to the coach in virtual reality. If it goes okay, Chris will have the courage to try it in real reality.

The rest of the week is very, very interesting. Chris and Chloe each take a few more trips to the past with their grandparents' DNA. They'll never think of their family the same way they used to. Everyone was young once, and now Chris and Chloe can actually picture it.

Even Grandma, who still doesn't trust the virtual reality time machine, decides to give it another try. Roscoe, their next-door neighbor's dog, always barks like crazy when he sees Grandma and Grandpa's blue Toyota. If they want to get any sleep at night, they have to keep it in the garage.

Grandpa says, "Roscoe must have had a bad experience as a puppy with a blue car, a Toyota, or a blue Toyota."

Grandma thinks it happened the day he brought the car home. She wasn't there, but she has a feeling Grandpa missed the driveway and almost ran over Roscoe. Grandpa still sometimes misses the driveway.

Grandma, who's very organized, finds the receipt for the car with the exact date they bought it. She gets Roscoe to lick a slide (he licks everything), then goes to Roscoe's past to wait outside for Grandpa to drive the car home that day.

Chris and Chloe's parents come home from their week in the empty part of Bolivia. It was a crazy experience, but they survived it together without any devices. They'll talk about it for years and they'll keep taking vacations, sometimes without their iPhones and sometimes without Chris and Chloe, who don't mind, because they can't wait to spend another week with their grandparents.

The movie ends with Chris and Chloe back home. We see them in school trying to collect DNA samples from April and the coach without them knowing it.

I like this movie idea. I wrote down a few notes so I'll remember it. I can't believe how much time passed since I came upstairs after dinner. Time for bed. I can't wait until tomorrow.

chapter 23

I woke up thinking about Chris and Chloe and their parents and grandparents. It's amazing. I know them now, and before last night they didn't even exist.

It was weird being in school. No one knows that later today I have a meeting with one of the biggest movie companies in the world.

The day was going so slowly that I told Mr. Knapp I have to leave history fifteen minutes early for a yearbook thing. I actually don't. I try not to do this too often, but today I thought even a little less history would help.

Mr. Hollander was in the Publication Room. I wanted to tell him about my meeting, but I would feel bad if I tell someone else before I tell my parents.

School was finally over. "Hey, Ethan!" He was on his way home. "Do you have a few minutes?"

"For what? Acting school?"

"No. No more acting. I want to tell you an idea I have for a movie." I wanted to practice. We walked to a playground a few blocks away. I pointed to a bench. "Why don't you sit there."

"Where are you gonna sit?"

"I'm not. I'm gonna stand." I wanted him to be able to see my face while I'm telling it, like the people in Los Angeles will later.

It took about eight minutes. I kept watching Ethan to see if he looked bored. I couldn't really tell. I finished, and it was very quiet.

Sometimes I think I know what people are thinking. But with Ethan, I have no idea. It was *so* quiet. Then he finally said something.

"I like it."

"You do?" He nodded. "What exactly do you like about it?"

"What do I like about it?" He thought for a

few seconds. "It's good."

"Oh. Okay. Good." I was thinking of more questions to ask him, but then he asked me one.

"Does Chris have a girlfriend?"

"No. Wait. I actually never thought about that." I thought about it. "Yes! He *does* have a girlfriend." I pulled out my notebook and started writing down a new part of the story with Chris's girlfriend so I would remember it. Ethan got up and walked away. "Ethan! Thanks!"

I finished writing down the idea and started walking home when I got a text.

We

It's Buzz. Should I go play Wii with him? If I go home, I'll just sit in my room and get nervous about the meeting. Everything is ready. Skype is working. I printed out my notes. I won't be able to read them on my computer during the meeting, because I'll be on Skype. I guess I actually *can* play Wii for a little while.

Nah. Nothing against Buzz, but it's a big day for me, and I don't want to spend part of it playing Wii, which I don't even like that much. And it won't be much fun being with a friend, not talking about the only thing I'm thinking about.

Not today but soon.

I went home, but I didn't even go into the house. I dropped my knapsack in the garage and got my bike. I rode to this little waterfall. Actually, it's not a real waterfall, just a place where water falls from one level down to another. It's pretty and I like the sound. I sat on the ground next to my bike for a while. I started throwing rocks into the water, but then I thought there might be fish in there, so I stopped.

When I got back, my dad was home from work. My mom is at the hospital. She's working an extra shift tonight. When my mom works the evening shift, my dad and I almost always have pizza for dinner. We both love pizza, and when it's just us, we don't have to have a salad, which is what makes it okay for my mom to have pizza for dinner.

Dad doesn't care what time we eat. When I asked him if we can make it a little later tonight, he was actually happy, because his favorite thing with pizza is TV and there's a show we like at eight. Eating in front of the TV is another thing that wouldn't happen if mom was home. Dad said he'll time the pizza order so we'll have our trays open in front of the set with hot pizza at eight.

I went upstairs to get my room ready for my Skype meeting. While I was sitting by the waterfall, I thought of a few other things I have to do. Like taking pictures of myself with my computer facing different directions, because with Skype they see you and they also see some of whatever is behind you.

My room is okay, though seeing it in these pictures makes me think it's time to get some new posters. You can love something when you're eleven, and you put up a poster for it, and then two years later you don't hate it exactly, but you don't want it on your wall anymore. And you definitely don't want it in the background for your Skype meeting.

I'm not one of those kids who looks in the mirror all the time. I know what I look like, more or less, and looking at it a lot doesn't do much for me. I can't really explain it. But since I just took five pictures of myself with my computer to pick the right background for the meeting, I got five chances to look at myself. I'm glad I did. There was a little piece of lunch on my shirt, so I changed.

I could comb my hair, but what would be the point? After a few minutes, it just goes back to looking however it wants to. My skin is okay. So far. My dad says, "Just wait."

Skype is working fine. Since Brad gave me their Skype address, I guess I'm supposed to Skype them. The meeting is at 5 PM their time. So when it's exactly 5:00 in Los Angeles I'll Skype them. Not before. Not after. Some people are always late for things and some people are always early, but to me, if you decide on a time together, that's the time.

I put my digital voice recorder on the desk next to my computer. I'm recording our meeting. I want to remember everything I tell them and everything they say. I may be so excited that I'll forget parts of it. I usually have a good memory, but you never know.

The other reason is that if *A Week with Your Grandparents* becomes a real movie, the recording of the meeting when I first told the story to the company might be a cool special feature on the DVD. It will only be a sound recording, but we can show scenes from the actual movie while I'm talking about them.

I thought about telling Stefanie I'm recording our meeting, but I decided not to. They know I record things. Dan Welch told her about my podcasts. She must have watched some of them by now. Maybe that's what convinced her to have the meeting.

There's nothing left to do. Everything is ready. Watching the numbers change on the clock on my computer, it seemed like the last three minutes were each longer than a minute. I was getting my stopwatch to check this, when I heard an e-mail come into Dan Welch's inbox. I left his account open in case they needed to tell us something. They better not be canceling.

Wait! It's not an e-mail. It's a chat.

Hey Dan Welch! Its Dan Welch!

It's Collectibles Dan Welch. I don't know what to do. I can't chat with anyone right now.

Hows your day going, buddy?

It was going okay until now.

Hey, I just sold a Michael Jackson cookie jar. Thats my next two car payments. Smile for me Dan Welch.

I tried to figure out what Management Dan Welch would do. He's not the kind of guy who ignores you if you're talking to him.

Wait! My computer clock says 5:02 Los Angeles time. I'm late for my meeting!

chapter 24

After only two of those funny Skype rings, they picked up. A guy came up on the screen. I wasn't sure at first, but he turned out to be Brad. I never thought about what Brad looks like, but it still felt like a surprise. He looks like he should be on *E! News* or *Entertainment Tonight*. His voice is like that, too.

BRAD: Is that Sean?
ME: Yeah, it is. Hi.
BRAD: I'm Brad. Nice to meet you.
          We've been in touch with
          Dan Welch.

I almost started laughing because I pictured the inside of our fridge.

ME: **I know. He told me.**

I suddenly remembered I spoke to Brad when I needed his e-mail address. Does he recognize my voice from that phone call? I can't think about it now. I can't try to change my voice.

BRAD: **Duh. That's why you Skyped us, right?**

I think maybe Brad said "Duh" because he was talking to a thirteen-year-old. I have actually never said the word "Duh."

ME: **Right.**
BRAD: **Okay, let me step aside and introduce you to everyone. This is Ashley, Devin, and Eva, our Directors of Development.**

They all crowded into the screen. I almost started laughing again. On Skype you see your own face on your screen, and seeing myself almost laugh made it worse.

ASHLEY: Hi, Sean.

DEVIN: Hi, Sean.

EVA: Hey, Sean.

ME: Hi.

Brad came back on the screen.

BRAD: And <u>this</u> is . . .

Now he sounds like he's announcing the winner of *American Idol*.

BRAD: Stefanie President.

She's pretty.

STEFANIE: Hi, Sean. I am so, so

**grateful you were able to
move up our meeting.**

It took me a minute to figure out what she was grateful for. Then I remembered that Dan asked if the meeting could be next week, but they wanted it to be *this* week.

Then she stood up. She's pregnant.

STEFANIE: **As you can see, I'm about to
pop. Oh no. Can I say that
to a thirteen-year-old?
Sorry, Sean. I'm new to this.
Children, I mean. Talking
to them and having them. It
feels like I've been pregnant
for nine years. It makes you
a little crazy. Anyway, if
you were sitting here with
us, this is when Brad would
offer you water.**

Brad stuck his head in.

BRAD: I started to. We're not used
            to having Skype meetings,
            Sean.

ME: Neither am I, actually.

STEFANIE: Good. So Sean, we've heard
            absolutely amazing things
            about you and your work.

From who? Dan Welch? Comments on my
podcasts?

ME: Did you see any of my
            podcasts?

STEFANIE: I had Brad bookmark them
            on my iPad and I can't
            wait to see them. Okay,
            Sean. We're all very excited
            to hear your idea.

ME: Oh good.

STEFANIE: So why don't you just start.

I told them the story of *A Week with Your
Grandparents*. I never looked at my notes, not

even for the new part. I remembered it all, and I even added things. Once I started talking, it just kept coming. It was like telling people what happened on the way to school yesterday.

When I finished, they were all quiet for what seemed like a really long time. It actually wasn't that long—5.2 seconds.

STEFANIE: Sean . . . You don't know me very well . . . so you don't know how unusual it is for me to say this . . . but . . . I like it.

ME: You do?

STEFANIE: Yes. It's absolutely adorable. When you started I thought, "Oh no, *Parental Guidance*," but it's nothing like that. (turns to the other people) What do you guys think?

They each took a turn on the screen.

ASHLEY: It's a family comedy, but the
           boy having the hots for his
           grandmother makes it edgy.

DEVIN: It's *Back to the Future*
           meets *Nanny McPhee*.

EVA: No. It's *17 Again* meets *The
           Bucket List*.

Stefanie came back on.

ME: Um . . . I actually haven't
           seen all those movies, but
           . . . I'm pretty sure it
           isn't like *The Bucket List*.

STEFANIE: You're right. It's new.
           Sean, thank you for bringing
           this to us. Has anyone else
           out here seen it?

ME: Actually, no.

STEFANIE: Good. I want this. Can you
           promise me you won't show
           it to anyone else? Remind
           me, who's your agent?

BRAD: (yells out) Dan Welch is
            his manager. I don't know
            who his agent is.

ME: I don't actually have an
            agent. Just Dan Welch.

STEFANIE: Well, we will definitely be
            in touch with Dan Welch.
            I'll be on maternity leave,
            and even though I won't
            be in the office, I'm always
            on my iPhone. Always. Think
            of me as Chris and Chloe's
            mom. But I live in
            Brentwood, not Bolivia, so
            you can always reach me.

ME: Oh good.

STEFANIE: I wish you were here, Sean,
            because I would give you the
            biggest hug. You're adorable.

ME: Thanks.

STEFANIE: Okay. We'll be in touch
            with . . . damn it . . .

                Sean, don't ever get
                pregnant. Brad, what was
                his agent's name again?

BRAD: (yells) His manager. Dan
                Welch.

STEFANIE: Right. Dan Welch. Bye, Sean.

didn't want the meeting to end. I probably never would have clicked on the little red Skype phone to hang up. They actually like my idea. I can't believe it. Well, I can, because *I* like my idea, but I didn't know if *they* would.

I want to Skype Stefanie again and tell her she's adorable, too. Adorable. What does that even mean? Adorable like a baby? Like a stuffed animal?

By the way, maybe you don't know this. In other countries, they don't call them stuffed animals. When Javier heard me say that, he thought it was disgusting. "You mean an animal dies and you stuff it and put it on your bed?" In Argentina they call it a *peluche*, which you have to admit is a better name.

It was actually a relief to think about Javier and stuffed animals for a minute, because thinking about the meeting was just too much. What would Javier say if he knew I might have just sold my movie to the company that made some of the biggest movies of all time, movies you probably saw and you definitely heard of, even in Argentina. The Vice President of Production actually said to me, "I want this."

How can you tell if you're dreaming something or if it's real? I've heard of people pinching themselves to see if they were awake. I don't like being pinched, even by myself. And why wouldn't you be able to pinch yourself in a dream? You still wouldn't know if you were actually awake or just dreaming you were awake.

Then I remembered. The digital voice recorder. It's still recording. I stopped it. I'm almost afraid to play it back.

I didn't dream the meeting. It really happened. Unless listening to the recording of the meeting is also part of my dream.

For some reason, I don't sound nervous on the

recording. Maybe my podcasts are good practice. Telling it to Ethan definitely helped.

I checked Dan Welch's e-mail to see if Stefanie or Brad or Ashley or Devin or Eva sent him an e-mail about our meeting. No one did. But the meeting was only a few minutes ago.

It was time to go downstairs for pizza with my dad. Sure enough, he had the TV trays set up, and he had our favorite drinks ready, a Coke in a bottle for me and a beer in a bottle for him. He had our first pieces of pizza ready on paper plates, which we use when my mom's not eating with us. My mom likes to have something healthy on pizza, like broccoli, but Dad doesn't care. Well, actually he *does* care. "The only vegetable that belongs on pizza is tomato sauce."

The TV show was starting so we didn't talk for a while. That was actually good. I was hungry and I was glad to stop thinking about you-know-what.

When the commercials started, my dad muted the TV. My mom just lets the commercials play. I probably would, too. I kind of like commercials, partly because I like to know about new things, but partly because I just like commercials. I wonder what the commercial for *A Week with Your Grandparents* will be.

It was quiet in the room with the TV muted.

"How's life, Seany?"

"Pretty good."

"Good." We got our second slices of pizza.

If my mom was here, she would be all over me. She would know as soon as I came downstairs that something is going on. She'd turn off the TV and say, "Okay. What is it?"

I hate to say it, but I'm glad she's working. I'm not ready to talk about it yet. I feel a little bad sitting here with my dad and not telling him.

When the next set of commercials came on, my dad muted the TV again. This time I asked *him* a question.

"Did you used to watch TV with your dad?"

"No, Seany. He wasn't home much at night. Another slice?"

We don't usually talk about my grandfather. When my dad got back from the kitchen, I decided to keep going. "Where was he at night?"

"I don't know, really. Working, I guess. He was very ambitious. Too ambitious."

I guess you could say I'm ambitious, too. If my dad knew what I've been doing, would he think I'm too ambitious? "What was Grandpa's job exactly?"

"We never exactly knew, Seany. Something with stocks or bonds. Something shady."

I knew my grandfather got into some kind of big trouble, but I never knew what kind of trouble. Like I said, no one ever talks about him. I wonder what my dad means by "shady." Is making up a manager so an entertainment company will talk to me shady? Is there a chance *I'll* get into big trouble?

I had a million more questions for my dad, but I think this conversation was making both of us nervous, so I went back to eating pizza and my dad unmuted the TV.

chapter 26

After the TV show, I went upstairs and spent the next four hours watching those movies that Devin and Eva said my movie is like. They're so wrong. In *Back to the Future*, Marty goes to the past, but he can actually change history. Chris and Chloe can't change anything except the way they think about things from now on.

Marty doesn't have a crush on his grandmother like Chris in my movie. In *Back to the Future* Marty's mom has a crush on *him*. She keeps touching him and trying to kiss him. It's gross, actually. Marty's parents are pretty scary in the present and also in the past. In my movie we laugh at Chris and Chloe's parents and how in love they are with their iPhones, but we like them. And we know that the things that happen to them in the movie will change the way *they* think about things, too.

I guess I didn't see *17 Again*, because I remember movies really well, and I don't remember this one at all. Mike is a dad with two teenaged kids. He's kind of a failure. He's getting divorced and he's not getting promoted at his job. He jumps into the water one day for some reason, and he gets turned into himself at seventeen.

His body is seventeen, but in his mind, he's still thirty-seven. The movie is funny sometimes, but there are things that make it hard to believe. Now that Mike is seventeen again, he looks exactly the same as the first time he was seventeen. But his wife, who was his girlfriend back then, doesn't recognize him. Mike is missing and there's this new guy who looks exactly like Mike used to look, but she doesn't know it's Mike. Neither do his kids. His daughter gets a crush on him and tries to kiss him, and his son becomes his best friend. Didn't these kids ever see a picture of their dad?

Back to the Future and *17 Again* are about people

getting another chance to fix something that didn't work out the first time. My movie is about looking at someone you thought you knew and finding out you actually didn't know them. Your grandparents were once kids just like you, and maybe even kids you would have really liked.

I don't think anyone turns into a whole new person when they get old. Maybe the reason they're so annoying now is they're mad they're not young anymore. Grandpa's virtual reality time machine doesn't let you change history. It just lets you see it.

My mom got home from work at about one in the morning. I heard her car drive up. I was in bed watching *The Bucket List*. I was only using one earbud so I'd be able to hear her. I quickly put my laptop under the covers so it would look like my room was dark and I was asleep. I paused the movie just in case.

I heard her come into the house. Usually when she comes home from working at night, she likes to eat something and have a drink. Like an alcohol drink.

I put the other earbud back in and started the movie again. A few minutes later, I felt this very light tapping on the top of my head, which was covered by the blanket. I took the earbuds out. "If it's bright enough for you to see under the covers, it's bright enough for me to see from the driveway. Also from under your door. Just for future reference." I took the covers off my head. "What are you watching?"

"*The Bucket List.*"

"Don't worry. We're not making you stay with Grandma." *The Bucket List* is about old people.

"Mom . . . do I remind you of Grandpa? Not your dad. Dad's." I was actually scared to hear her answer.

"No, Sean. You're nothing like Grandpa." She sat down next to me on the bed. "Why did you ask me that?"

"I don't know. Who do I remind you of?"

"Sean Rosen."

That answer is so my mom. "Was Grandpa the one who didn't want you and Dad to get married?"

My mom laughed. "The *one*? One of four. It

was unanimous. None of them thought we should get married."

"Why were they like that? That makes me mad at them."

"No, sweetie. Don't blame them. I didn't. We were very young. Even though your dad and I were a couple for three years and we had our own apartment, he was still only twenty-two and I was twenty-one. We were just graduating from college."

"Well, *you* were."

"Right. Though it felt like your dad graduated, too. He was there the whole time. Except for classes."

"Did your parents like Dad?"

"They really didn't *get* him. A lot of people didn't back then." She thought for a few seconds. "I always got him."

"Did the Rosens get *you*?"

"Not really, but they thought I was good for him. And even though they never met anyone like me and I never met anyone like them, we always just . . . liked one another. They came to my graduation, even though your dad didn't finish."

"If they liked you, why didn't they want you to get married?"

"Sean . . . the Rosens had a lot going on back then. And no one believed your dad was ready to settle down. No one except me. But I'm leaving out part of the story. One big reason none of them wanted us to get married . . . was that we did it right after graduation."

"What's wrong with that?"

My mom looked embarrassed. "I mean *right* after graduation. The wedding was three hours later. We planned it that way so our parents would all be there. But we didn't tell them the plan until graduation was over."

"That afternoon was the first time you ever mentioned it?" She nodded. I thought about it. "That actually explains a lot."

"We never regretted it, Sean."

"Did everyone come?

"Everyone? Yeah, our parents and the three other people we invited. It wasn't much fun. We just . . . had to do it. Wait! I don't mean we *had* to do it. I mean, I wasn't . . ."

"I got it, Mom."

"We both just really wanted to be married. And we didn't want a big fuss."

"I guess you guys deserve a new honeymoon."

She kissed me good night. "Put the laptop away."

The door closed. My pillow felt so good. What an amazing day. Mom, I'm sorry. You told me so much interesting stuff tonight, and I didn't tell you that in this very room, while you were at work, I sold my first movie to Hollywood. Maybe.

At school the next day I kept thinking that this was Stefanie V. President's last day of work before going on maternity leave. Before she pops. I once actually saw a video of a baby being born, and when it came out, it didn't exactly pop. I didn't see every second of it because I covered my eyes part of the time.

Did Stefanie really like my movie, or was she just being nice to a kid? She said she would definitely be in touch with Dan Welch. Wait a minute. What if she wants to call him? There was no phone number in his e-mail to her. He doesn't *have* a phone number.

What if she asks Brad to Google Dan Welch

Management to get his phone number? He doesn't have a website. Dan Welch Management won't even come up on Google. But Collectibles Dan Welch might. I'm glad his website is UNameitIGotit.com and not DanWelch.com

Even if I wanted to get a phone number for Dan Welch, I can't. You have to have your own credit card. A lot of kids do, but I don't. Then you have to go somewhere to get the phone and the phone number, and someone over twenty-one has to actually sign something. It's not like on the internet, when they ask if you're over eighteen and you say yes, and nobody ever checks. So if Stefanie wants to call Dan, she won't be able to.

I just thought of something else. That time I called Brad pretending I was Dan Welch's assistant, I said my name was Chris. Chris is also the name of the kid in *A Week with Your Grandparents*. I can't believe I did that.

I wonder if Brad figured it out. I actually don't think so. I'm not saying he isn't smart, but at the beginning of the Skype meeting, he acted as nervous as I was. Actually, I think they were all a little nervous. Maybe everyone gets nervous.

The day went by very, very slowly. History felt like it lasted a century. Mr. Knapp is always boring, but today, as my grandmother (Thorny) would say, "He outdid himself."

Then there was French. *Merde!* (I'm not going to translate that.) Mademoiselle Fou decided we would read out loud today. We do that sometimes, usually from the textbook. Last year we read *Le Petit Prince* (*The Little Prince*). Today she said we're going to read the first chapter of a book by a French writer named Marcel Proust.

Mademoiselle Fou handed out copies that she made herself from the original book. She used a paperback, and she obviously doesn't know how to enlarge things. Each page of the copy had a lot of empty space, and then in one corner, a copy of the small paperback book, with tiny writing.

Brianna was whispering something to me, and I suddenly hear, "Gaston, why don't you begin." She was talking to me. Gaston is my French name. Everyone has to have a French name. In my row, Aurora is Celine, Jeremy is Remie, and I'm Gaston.

I was shocked that Mademoiselle Fou called on me. I didn't even raise my hand. I started to read, and she said, *"Ici." Ici* means "here." She was pointing to the front of the room. We usually read from our seats. I hate it when I have to stand in front of twenty-five kids I know.

It's different when you're in front of the whole school in a show, like *Le Bistro* last year. Completely different. The auditorium is dark and there are bright lights shining on you. You can't even see the audience. Plus in *Le Bistro* it wasn't *me* up there. I was playing a character. Plus I knew I was doing a show that day. I rehearsed. I was ready. Today was a sneak attack.

So I'm standing there, and I look at the first sentence of the book. I never heard of Marcel Proust, but he (or she) uses a lot of French words I never saw before. I can't completely see them now, because besides the words being so small, it looks like Mademoiselle Fou took the book off the copy machine before it was finished copying. So some of the words are s t r e t c h e d   o u t.

She also didn't open the book wide enough,

so the words look like they're falling into the crack. You can't always tell what the first letter of a line is.

I asked Mademoiselle Fou if she had Marcel Proust's actual book with her. She said, *"Pourquoi?"* ("Why?") I told her the copy was a little hard to read. She said, *"La vie n'est pas facile."* ("Life isn't easy.") A few kids laughed. Most of them didn't know what she said.

I started reading, and after every word she interrupted me and said, *"Non."* ("No.") Then she said the word I just said, correcting my pronunciation. Sometimes I had a feeling that *I* was right and *she* was wrong, but I didn't say that, because I wasn't completely sure. What really got me mad was when she stopped me and then pronounced the word exactly the same way *I* did. After the third time, I couldn't take it anymore.

"That's what I just said!"

A couple of kids went, "Ooooh" and Jeremy said, "Uh oh." Mademoiselle Fou looked at me for a few seconds, then she said, *"Tu as tort. Assieds-toi."* ("You are wrong. Sit down.") I sat down, and after that she didn't make anyone else try to read Marcel Proust.

I didn't feel like I did anything wrong, but I was still embarrassed. It was like your friends' parents fighting in front of you, except it was *me*.

How did this happen? How can the best day of my life be followed by one of the worst? I want to go home, but I don't have the energy to pretend I'm sick. After French I went to hide in the Publication Room, but there was an editors' meeting for the school newspaper. I waved to Brianna. She's the fashion editor. The newspaper never had a fashion editor before, but Brianna talked them into it. She waved back, then made a sad face. She knows the whole Mademoiselle Fou story.

Part of me wants to check Dan Welch's e-mail. My phone doesn't have e-mail, but there are lots of other ways—other kids' phones, the library, Trish in the principal's office.

But I don't want to sign in to Dan Welch's e-mail account on anyone else's phone or computer. I'm pretty sure it keeps a record, even if it says it doesn't. The bigger thing is that I don't want to feel any worse than I already do, and if there's nothing from Stefanie to Dan, I definitely will. I don't even want to go home, because I'll just stare at Dan Welch's inbox.

chapter 28

We're not supposed to text during school, but everyone does. I usually don't, but it feels a little like an emergency. I looked to see if any teachers were around, and holding my phone inside my locker, I texted Buzz.

Play wii today?

He got back to me in about ten seconds.

shur comm over

Some people make up strange spellings to be funny or cool. Not Buzz. I'm not saying he's not funny or cool, but he spells that way all the time. His parents keep thinking it's the school's fault. They took him out of our school and put him in a different school. Then they didn't like *that* school, so they found another one. Buzz still can't spell, but he doesn't hate school anymore. I don't think they have to spell in his new school. And they take a lot of trips.

I actually don't think it matters which school Buzz goes to. It's just Buzz. He never completely listens to anything. Not in a mean way. It's like part of his brain is in some other place. He's always been like that. Sometimes I think it's funny that a kid like me and a kid like him are friends. We've never been like best friends, but I always liked him and he always liked me.

It'll be fun to see Buzz, and today I'm actually looking forward to Wii baseball. I'm not very good at it, so I have to concentrate really hard, which means I can't think about Mademoiselle Fou or Stefanie V. President.

After three innings Buzz was ahead 19-0. If there was a game that I knew I was always going to win, I'm not sure I'd want to keep playing, but Buzz doesn't seem to mind. We decided to take a break to have a snack.

Buzz's house is the snack capital of the world.

Besides their regular refrigerator and freezer, they have a whole separate freezer with every possible snack you could ever want. I'm not kidding. They have pizza, ice cream, tacos, onion rings, mini-burgers, fries, frozen candy bars . . . everything. Buzz and I microwaved some chicken and cheese burritos and got some Cokes. The last time I was over he asked me if I wanted a beer, and I didn't. He didn't ask this time.

We went back to Buzz's room, and after we had our snacks, Buzz picked up his guitar and started playing. He doesn't actually play songs, at least songs you ever heard of, but it always sounds pretty good. I wasn't going to do this, but I asked if I could use his computer for a minute.

I signed in to Dan Welch's e-mail account. Buzz's computer asked me if I wanted it to remember the password. I said no, of course. Actually, I can't imagine Buzz ever wanting to read someone else's e-mail. I don't think he ever reads his own.

There was one e-mail in Dan's inbox. It was from Stefanie V. President.

To: Dan Welch Management
From: Stefanie V. President

Dear Dan,

We LOVE Sean. He's absolutely adorable. If I weren't giving birth in the next millisecond, I would adopt him.

We loved his pitch, and we want to option his idea. I'm going on maternity leave today, but you'll be hearing from business affairs early next week. We want this to happen. If you need me, just e-mail me. I'll get back to you even if I'm screaming in pain squeezing out Marisa. That's her name. We had to pick one three months ago when we filled out her preschool application.

Thanks for bringing this project to us, Dan. We'll do it right and make a movie we're all proud of.

Dilating as we speak,

Stefanie

Oh. My. God. I actually said this out loud. When you're alone a lot, you never know for sure if you're thinking something or actually saying it.

Buzz stopped playing and said, "What?"

Buzz doesn't usually ask people questions. It took me by surprise. I thought for a minute. Do I want to tell him? I don't want to show him the e-mail, so I signed out of Dan Welch's account. I started to clear the history on Buzz's browser, but then I remembered it's not my computer. Buzz might have some websites he wants to remember.

I thought he would just go back to playing the guitar, but he didn't. I didn't have my digital voice recorder with me, but I'm pretty sure I remember our conversation.

BUZZ: What?!
ME: Do you really want to know?
BUZZ: Know what?
ME: What I'm so happy about.
BUZZ: I just asked you, didn't I?
ME: Yes. You did. Do you promise not to tell anyone?

BUZZ: Tell anyone what?

ME: What I'm about to tell you.

BUZZ: What are you about to tell me?

ME: Nothing, unless you promise not to tell anyone.

BUZZ: Who am I gonna tell?

ME: I don't know. It's kind of cool. You might want to tell people.

BUZZ: I doubt it. If you're gonna tell me, tell me. I gotta take a leak.

ME: Go ahead.

BUZZ: So you're <u>not</u> gonna tell me?

ME: Maybe when you get back.

BUZZ: Now or never.

ME: Why?

BUZZ: Forget it.

He went to the bathroom. He came back.

ME: I should get going.

BUZZ: I thought you wanted to play Wii.

ME: I did. We did.

BUZZ: You're done?

ME: I guess.

BUZZ: Because I had to take a leak?

ME: No.

BUZZ: Because of whatever happened on
        the computer?

ME: Maybe.

BUZZ: What <u>was</u> it?

I actually don't blame him for being annoyed. I was being annoying.

ME: Okay. You know _____? (the
        enormous entertainment company where
        Stefanie works)

BUZZ: Do I <u>know</u> them?

ME: I know you don't know them, but
        you've heard of them, right?

BUZZ: I guess. I don't know.

ME: Forget it.

BUZZ: What about them?

ME: I can't believe you never heard

of them. They're huge. They're
the company that made _____,
_____ and _____. (three of the
biggest movies ever—everyone saw them,
everyone.)

BUZZ: They must be rich.

ME: Well, yeah. Anyway, I had an
idea for a movie and they want
to buy it.

BUZZ: Really?

ME: Yeah.

BUZZ: How do they even know about it?

ME: Well . . . Do you promise not
to tell anyone?

BUZZ: Not <u>this</u> again.

ME: They think I have a manager.

BUZZ: A what?

ME: A manager. It's like an agent
but different. Anyway, they
only had a meeting with me
because my manager wrote to
them and set it up.

BUZZ: Okay. So what's the big secret?

ME: I don't actually have a
        manager. It's actually me. I
        wrote to them and pretended I
        was this manager named Dan
        Welch.

BUZZ: Have they ever seen you?

ME: Yes. We had a meeting on Skype.

BUZZ: Then why do they think you're a
        manager?

ME: They saw *me*, Sean Rosen, on
        Skype. I'm the one with the
        idea. They only got e-mails
        from my manager.

BUZZ: And they want to buy your idea?

ME: Yes.

BUZZ: I didn't know you could sell
        ideas.

ME: Well, you can. Now I have to
        write the screenplay, and then
        they'll make it into a movie,
        and then it will be a lot more
        than an idea.

Buzz thought for a little while.

BUZZ: I have an idea. Do you think Dan Walters can sell it for me?

ME: It's Dan Welch. Like the grape juice.

BUZZ: Whatever. Can you ask him if he'll sell it for me?

ME: There's no him to ask. Ask me.

BUZZ: Ask you what?

ME: Nothing. Never mind.

BUZZ: What don't you want me to tell anyone?

ME: Nothing. Just forget it.

chapter 29

I got home from Buzz's and my mom was there. I forgot she was off today.

"Hi, handsome."

"Why do you call me that?"

"Because you are."

"No, I'm not. And when you say I am, it makes me wonder if the other nice things you say about me are true."

"It's all true, Sean. What's new?" If I was smart, I would have told *her* my good news instead of Buzz. I wanted to go upstairs and read Stefanie's e-mail again, but my mom was in the mood to talk. "So . . . *The Bucket List*. What did you think?"

"This isn't a trick question, is it?"

"What do you mean?"

"I turned it off right when you said to."

"Okay. But what do you think of it so far?"

"Mom, you know I don't like to talk about something until I see the whole thing."

"You *want* to see the whole thing?"

"You didn't like it, right?"

"I didn't say that."

"You think the hospital in the movie is too fake. They don't have curtains between the beds, right?"

"I thought you didn't want to talk about it."

"I don't, actually."

"Okay. How was school?"

"How was school?" I didn't feel like telling her about Mademoiselle Fou. I don't want to think about it anymore. "School . . . was about four hours too long. For example, why do we have to eat lunch there? I would rather eat anywhere else in the universe. And *no* one can pay attention for six hours, even if every one of your subjects and every one of your teachers is really interesting. Which unfortunately never happens. School should be two and a half hours a day."

She looked at me for a second. "Really?"

"Yes, really. You know it's true. You weren't in school *that* long ago."

"Thanks, sweetie."

I kissed her on the cheek and ran upstairs.

I opened Dan Welch's account and read the e-mail again. I pretended I was reading it for the first time.

To: Dan Welch Management
From: Stefanie V. President

Dear Dan,

We LOVE Sean. He's absolutely adorable. If I weren't giving birth in the next millisecond, I would adopt him.

We loved his pitch, and we want to option his idea. I'm going on maternity leave today, but you'll be hearing from business affairs early next week. We want this to happen. If you need me, just e-mail me. I'll get back to

you even if I'm screaming in pain squeezing out Marisa.
That's her name. We had to pick one three months ago
when we filled out her preschool application.

Thanks for bringing this project to us, Dan. We'll do it
right and make a movie we're all proud of.

Dilating as we speak,

Stefanie

I like it even better the second time. My life
just changed. I'm in the movie business. One of
the biggest entertainment companies in the world
is going to make my movie.

All across the United States . . . No. All over
Planet Earth, a year or two from now, when you
pass a movie theater, this is what you'll see on the
sign: A WEEK WITH YOUR GRANDPARENTS.

Wait. Is the name too long? Will they have to
shorten it for the sign? To what? WEEK GRAND-
PARENTS? People who can't spell will think the
name of the movie is WEAK GRANDPARENTS. That

doesn't sound very interesting.

Maybe they'll just put GRANDPARENTS on the sign. That doesn't sound like much fun either. Maybe some people won't go because they don't like spending time with their own grandparents. Why would they pay to be with someone else's?

But people will already know about the movie from TV and the internet. And there'll be movie stars in it. I'm actually going to meet movie stars. I'm probably going to be on *E!* I guess I always thought I would be, but I didn't think it would be so soon.

Will I have to move to Los Angeles? Was today my last day at my school? Am I going to be rich? Should I get different clothes?

Stefanie V. President is going to laugh when she hears about that stupid letter her company sent me saying I stole their idea, when I never even told them the idea. I wonder if I should tell her that we only got in touch with her as a trial run. And that when Dan wrote and told her I had a movie idea, I actually didn't. Now I do, and you know what? It actually *can* be a whole series of movies.

"Sean! Telephone!" It had to be Javier. He was calling to invite me over for dinner. I really like Javier's family. They think I'm funny and I think they're funny, which is cool because I don't speak Spanish and they don't speak much English. They like me to come over so they can practice.

They mostly eat the foods they ate in Argentina, and unfortunately, I can never tell from looking at something if I'm going to like it or not. It makes me nervous, because I don't want to hurt Javier's mom's feelings if I don't. I'm not very good at eating things I don't like.

I told Javier that I have to have dinner with my parents, but I can come over for dessert. I learned this from my mom. Sometimes when we're invited for dinner and she either doesn't like the person's cooking or knows we don't want to spend too much time with them, she suggests that we come for dessert. My dad says, "Good work, Leecie (her name is Elise). You should run for president."

Javier's mom said okay. I'm glad. I almost never have to worry if I'm going to like dessert.

I read Stefanie's e-mail again. "We want to

option his idea." What does that mean? Doesn't she mean, "We want to *make* his movie"?

I guess at this point it actually *is* only an idea. I can see the whole movie, even parts of it I didn't tell them yet. But at some point I have to write it all down, so the actors will know exactly what to say and do when we start shooting.

We also have to pick a director. I spent the next hour making a list of directors that I like. I wonder if I should include directors whose movies I like even if their movies are nothing like *A Week with Your Grandparents*? Like if you directed a really good animated movie, could you direct my movie?

Maybe *A Week with Your Grandparents* should be animated. It could be. Maybe more people would go to see it. It doesn't really sound like the name of an animated movie, but neither did *Up*.

There are a lot of things for Stefanie and me to think about.

chapter 30

I was glad I was with Javier's family last night because it took my mind off waiting to hear from business affairs. Plus the dulce de leche. Try it some time. It's my new favorite dessert.

I should watch the rest of *The Bucket List* so I can talk to my mom about it, and so I can figure out why Eva said my movie is like *17 Again* meets *The Bucket List*. Last night I got to where the two old guys know they're dying, so they might as well do what they always wanted to do. Unfortunately, it took them forever in that hospital room without a curtain to figure it out, and I just can't spend another minute with them.

I think the only thing about *The Bucket List*

that's like my movie is there are old people in it. I watched *Nanny McPhee* instead. At first it seemed like it was for eight-year-olds, but I ended up liking it. Still, it doesn't remind me of my movie at all. I think Devin said *Nanny McPhee* because it's about someone taking care of someone else's kids. She does it with magic. In my movie there's no magic, just science. I think Eva and Devin both liked my movie, so they tried to compare it to other movies that lots of people saw.

If you have an idea, you don't really want people comparing it to someone else's idea. It's like saying you copied it. Stefanie didn't compare it to anything else. She said it's new. I think it is, too.

What I really want to do this weekend is work on YOUR GRANDPARENTS. That's my new short version of the name, which I like better than WEEK GRANDPARENTS or GRANDPARENTS. But since I promised everyone a new podcast, I have to work on the bar mitzvah.

I was going to edit part one this week and part two next week, but it turns out it's easier to work on both at the same time. That's good, because next week might be very busy with the movie. Things are moving faster than I ever thought they would.

Listening to my grandmother at the bar mitzvah, I suddenly remembered the e-mail I sent her. I've been checking Dan Welch's e-mail constantly, but I never look at my own. Grandma actually wrote back to me three minutes after getting my e-mail five days ago.

To: Sean Rosen
From: Thorny Rosen

Dear Sean,

I was extremely disappointed to hear that you won't be using my interview. In my opinion, it was "pure gold," and it would have added a "special something" to your podcast. I'll consider what you suggested about withholding your present. It's a long time until your birthday. We'll see. Perhaps I'll heal by then.

Love and knishes,
Grandma

She reminds me a little of Chris and Chloe's grandmother.

I wonder if I'll keep doing podcasts now that I'm making movies. I may not have time. And I may think they're not important enough. I hope I don't feel that way. Podcasts were the way I got started, even though Stefanie decided to buy my movie without ever seeing my podcasts. I wonder if Marisa has been born yet. I wonder if Stefanie is watching one of my podcasts on her iPad right now.

Wait a minute. If she loved my movie without ever seeing my podcasts, I wonder if watching them now will make her change her mind about the movie.

I stopped working on my bar mitzvah podcast and I started watching all the other podcasts on my website. I tried to figure out if there's anything in them that will make Stefanie stop thinking I'm adorable and stop wanting to make my movie.

I decided I was being crazy, and got back to work on the bar mitzvah podcasts. I finished at about two in the morning. I didn't have to stop to eat because it was Saturday and my parents had a date.

Sunday my parents and I all had a day off. My dad made breakfast. He's always in a good mood after date night. They both are. He made French toast and bacon. It was delicious. The French toast had an orange flavor, and my dad really knows how to cook bacon. Some Jewish people don't eat bacon, but he does and I do.

We decided to go out to a movie. I love going to the movies in the afternoon. Well, I love going to the movies any time, but during the day is extra fun for some reason. Picking a movie is never easy. None of us will just see anything.

I'm leaving out the names of the movies here, because soon I might be working with the companies that made them, either on my movie or on my big idea. I know I already talked about some movies and said their names, but those were old ones.

MOM: So what should we see?
ME: _____ (an animated film that looks amazing). It's 3-D.

DAD: Sorry, Seany. Today I'm only good
for 2-Ds.

My mom looks at the newspaper.

MOM: It's also playing at a theater
that doesn't have 3-D.
ME: Why don't we just stay home and
watch it on the toaster oven.
MOM: Actually, I don't really want to
see that movie.
ME: Why not?
MOM: It doesn't matter, Sean. I don't
want to see it.
ME: Are you just saying that because
Dad doesn't want to see it?

My mom doesn't answer. She keeps looking at
the paper.

MOM: How about _____? (a movie that
takes place in some prairie)
DAD: What's that?

ME: It's a nature movie.

MOM: It's not a nature movie. It just takes place in a rural area. It got a very good review.

ME: Yeah. By the same guy who loved _____. (the worst movie ever made . . . we went because of the good review—my dad hated it, too)

DAD: We're not seeing that.

MOM: This movie has nothing to do with that movie.

DAD: Can I see the paper?

We ended up seeing a movie we all liked. My dad picked it out. It was the only movie in the paper that none of us already had an opinion about.

I wouldn't say a lot of things happened in this movie, but you really liked the person it was about. You had fun spending time with her.

That's what I want Chris and Chloe to be like. Like actual kids, but kids you really like. That's how I imagine them. In the movie we just saw, I believed everything the main character said and did. I know those things are written in the screen-play. But then the actress made it feel like she was a real person who was just saying and doing those things. It's so important to find the right actors. I want to talk about this with Stefanie at our next meeting.

"English is such a rich language, isn't that right, Javier?"

"*Sí,* Miss Meglis. *Muy rico.* Very rich."

"And yet . . . and yet . . . you would never suspect that from reading these." She held up our homework assignments. "If these tired paragraphs were your only exposure to our beautiful language, it would be sad indeed. Beyond sad. Unpatriotic. Please, ladies and gentlemen. Have pity on your humble teacher. Make your writing more interesting. Be descriptive. Be specific. Be colorful. Help me picture what you're writing about.

"For my sake, I will not ask you to read these. But I *will* give you one example." Then in a voice like a really bored kid, she read from one of our essays: "'Then we went to the store.'

"You're telling me *nothing* here." Then in an English accent she said, "To whom do you refer when you say 'we'? If you are like me, the Queen of England, one might use the word 'we' to refer to oneself. 'No, thank you, sire, *we* do not need to use the restroom before the royal wedding.'"

Then in her normal voice, "In this case, let's assume the author of 'Then we went to the store' is not using the royal 'we'. *Who* went? Two people? Three people? The entire cast of *Glee*? To picture this trip to the store, it would be helpful to know.

"'Then we went to the store.' You *went*. Did you walk? Did you drive? Did you float there in a hot air balloon? There are *no* clues in this sentence. Tell us so we can see it. Did you *stroll* to the store?" Miss Meglis strolled slowly across the front of the room. "Did you *dash* to the store?" She dashed. "Did you pirouette?"

Miss Meglis did a pirouette. She is not a dancer. When she spun around, she knocked Javier's glasses off his face and they went flying across the room.

They didn't break. Everyone cracked up, including Javier.

Javier loves Miss Meglis. She never makes him feel dumb for knowing less English than most of us. She sometimes gives him extra help after school.

Javier was one of the best students in his school in Argentina, so he gets frustrated here sometimes. But at least here, he's one of the best soccer players.

The bell rang in the middle of Brianna naming possible stores for "We went to the store."

When I was walking to school this morning, I saw Brianna getting out of her mom's car. She didn't see me. I started to say hi, but then I saw her face. She wasn't crying, but something was really bothering her. Brianna usually looks more grown up than most seventh graders, but today her face looked different—like a little girl.

Walking to our next class I thought about asking her if everything is okay, but I don't like when people ask me that, and she probably doesn't either. Especially when she's acting like her usual self. "Sean, should I redo my locker?"

This is one of those questions you don't really

need to answer. Brianna *will* redo her locker. Maybe not today. But soon.

I guess we're not going to talk about whatever it was this morning.

After school I rushed home because I wanted to see if anything arrived from Los Angeles. I ran up the stairs, I slipped, I spilled some apple juice, I wiped it up, I *walked* up the stairs. I finally got to my room and opened Dan Welch's e-mail.

I'm confused.

I'm not saying this to brag, but I'm usually pretty smart. I get good grades (unless I don't like the subject or the teacher). When anyone in my family gets a new phone or computer, I'm the one who figures out how it works. So why can't I understand the Option Agreement that Dan Welch got by e-mail from the business affairs department?

First of all, why do they call it the business affairs department? Why isn't it just the business department? What do they mean by "affairs"? My grandmother, after the bar mitzvah in Detroit, said, "Except for that horrible emcee, it was a lovely affair." Brianna told me that her mom had an affair because her dad had an affair. She wasn't talking about bar mitzvahs.

I was able to understand everything Stefanie V. President said at our meeting and wrote to Dan Welch, but this Option Agreement has whole pages that make no sense at all. If you think I'm exaggerating, try reading one paragraph. The blank parts are the name of the company.

This Agreement, including the terms contained in _____'s standard terms and conditions for an Artist incorporated herein by reference (subject only to such changes as may be mutually agreed in writing after good faith negotiations within _____'s standard parameters), contains the full and complete understanding between the parties and supersedes all prior agreements and understandings pertaining hereto and cannot be modified except by a writing signed by each party. Artist's sole and exclusive remedy for _____'s breach, termination, or cancellation of this Agreement or any term hereof (including any term pertaining to credit) shall be an action for damages and Artist irrevocably waives any right to equitable or injunctive relief.

If _____ exercises the option by written notice but unlawfully fails to pay Artist the Purchase Price set forth in Paragraph 2 above within a reasonable period of time after _____'s receipt of written notice from Artist of such a failure and provided _____ is not entitled to any legal right of offset or withholding of the Purchase Price, then the rights to the Property (excluding any material written by Artist as a work made for hire for _____) shall revert to the Artist.

There are forty pages of that. The only part I like is that they call me the Artist. I started to print it out, but we only have twenty-three pieces of paper. I tried to read it, I really did. It's impossible. They probably expect you to just give up and say "I Agree."

Here's what I can figure out. They'll pay me 500 dollars for the option of making a movie based on my idea. I looked up *option*. That means while they have the option I can't sell my movie to anyone else. So for 500 dollars they have three years to decide if they actually want to make my movie. If they still haven't decided, they can have two *more* years to think about it, if they give me another 500 dollars.

If they decide to make the movie, they'll "Purchase the Property" for 7,500 dollars, minus the 500 dollars (or 1,000 dollars) they already paid me. If they Purchase the Property, they own all rights to the plot, theme, title, characters, sequels, remakes, translations, and adaptations of my idea for motion pictures, television movies, television series, stage plays including musicals, books, merchandise, and theme park rides. They'll own these rights in perpetuity (that means forever) throughout the universe.

I think that means if I want to go on the *A Week with Your Grandparents* ride at a theme park on Mars in the year 2075, I have to pay just like everyone else, because they'll own it.

After that amazing Skype meeting, even after Stefanie's "We LOVE Sean" e-mail, I didn't think about how much money I would make. I was happy they liked my movie, and I was excited to be able to work on it with a big, successful entertainment company.

I knew it wouldn't be 100 million dollars, which is how much I think my big entertainment idea is worth. This is only one movie. But still, I never thought they would pay me so little.

I know how much money movies make. Everyone does, even if you don't read *The Hollywood Reporter*. It's in the newspaper, it's on TV, it's online. Movies from big companies like Stefanie's make millions of dollars, just in one weekend. And they cost millions of dollars to make. Why would the person who thought the whole thing up only get 7,500 dollars? It doesn't sound fair.

If they buy my idea, they own the characters. That makes me sad. It means I can't have any more ideas with Chris and Chloe. I like them. During history today I started thinking of another story with them.

And why do they need five years to decide if they want to make the movie? Stefanie said she wanted it five minutes after hearing it.

I don't understand any of this. On Friday I was like the happiest kid in the world and now I feel terrible.

chapter 32

I don't know what to do. I want to ask Dan Welch, but unfortunately I can't. I could ask my parents. They're both smart and they like movies, but they don't know anything about the movie business. They never want to read my *Hollywood Reporter.*

I know there are lawyers in my town, but I seriously doubt that any of them ever worked on an Option Agreement for a movie.

Wait! I just remembered. A few months ago there was an article about the best lawyers in the entertainment business. Fortunately, I save all my *Hollywood Reporter*s. I picked a law firm that sounds good and found their phone number on the internet.

It isn't as late in Los Angeles as it is where I live, so I hit "record" on my digital voice recorder and called them.

WOMAN: Pastrami, Salami, Baloney, and Hamm. (not their real name)

ME: Hi. I'm looking for a lawyer.

WOMAN: What's the lawyer's name?

ME: No. I mean I don't have one yet. I'm looking for one.

She waited 3.6 seconds, then she hung up.

I couldn't figure out why, so I called back.

WOMAN #2:   Pastrami, Salami, Baloney and Hamm.

ME: I'm looking for a lawyer to help me with a movie deal.

WOMAN #2:   Did someone refer you?

ME: No.

WOMAN #2:   How did you come to us?

ME: I read about you in the
           Hollywood Reporter.

After 2.4 seconds, she hung up.

What is it with these people? For some reason, I decided to call again. For three reasons,
actually. One, I don't like to give up. Two, if
they know I have a forty-page Option Agreement
from a huge famous company (everyone except
Buzz knows them—*you* know them), they might
at least talk to me about being my lawyer. And
three, it's easier to hit REDIAL than start all over
again.

WOMAN #1: Pastrami, Salami, Baloney
           and Hamm.
ME: This is Sean Rosen calling.
           _____ (the huge entertainment
           company) wants to option my
           movie idea. I'm looking for
           a lawyer to work with.
WOMAN #1: I'll connect you with one
           of our associates.

ME: A lawyer?
WOMAN #1:   Yes. He's an associate.
            His name is Jim Justice.
            (not his real name)
ME: Okay. Thanks.
WOMAN #1:   You're very welcome.

Suddenly they were nice to me. I don't think she remembered me from my first call, which was only fifteen minutes ago. The hold music was very relaxing.

ASSOCIATE: Hi, Sean. This is Jim
            Justice.
ME: Hi.
ASSOCIATE: You can call me Jim.
ME: Okay.
ASSOCIATE: So you're in business with
            _____ (the entertainment
            company)?
ME: Yeah. They want to option
            my idea.
ASSOCIATE: Cool. Who's your agent?

ME: Actually, I don't have an agent.

ASSOCIATE: How'd you get your idea to them?

ME: Oh. Actually . . .

Actually, I wanted to throw up.

ME: My manager got me the meeting.

ASSOCIATE: Who's that?

ME: Dan Welch.

ASSOCIATE: I don't know him.

ME: He's very good.

ASSOCIATE: He must be. Okay, let me tell you how we work. Our basic rate is six-fifty an hour . . .

I didn't know if he meant 650 dollars an hour or 6 dollars and 50 cents an hour, but they both seemed impossible, so I didn't say anything.

> ASSOCIATE: . . . and we require a ten-
>   thousand dollar retainer.

No one said anything for 8.1 seconds. That doesn't sound like a very long time, but next time you're having a conversation with someone, stop talking for 8.1 seconds. It's very long and very quiet.

ME: Retainer?
ASSOCIATE: You pay us ten thousand
            dollars before we start.
            That gives you fifteen
            hours and change. It's an
            advance.
ME: Could I just hire you for
            like a half hour?
ASSOCIATE: Funny. Okay, Sean, call if
            you decide you want to move
            forward with us. Good luck.

I put the phone down and laid on my bed. I felt like crying, but sometimes even when I want to, I don't. This was one of those times.

I don't understand. It costs 10,000 dollars for a lawyer, but I might only make 500 dollars from my movie. No. My movie *idea*. So far it's only an idea. To me it's a movie, but to them it's worth about the same as an iPad. There are millions of iPads, but there's only one *A Week with Your Grandparents*.

I don't know what to do. I could call Stefanie in the hospital, or wherever she is, and say, "You said you liked it. You said it was absolutely adorable. You said it was new. Here. Listen." Then I would play the recording of our meeting.

Then I would say, "Really? Five hundred dollars? Why don't you just send me an iPad?"

Then she would say, "I can't believe you recorded our meeting without asking me. That isn't how we work around here. And shouldn't you be complaining about all this to what's-his-name? Your manager?"

Then I would say, "I can't. Dan Welch is just someone I made up."

Then she would say, "You little liar. How dare

you? You wasted my time. You wasted Brad's time. You wasted Ashley, Devin, and Eva's time. Our business affairs department will be sending you a bill for all of *their* time that you wasted. That Option Agreement was forty pages, Sean. Maybe you don't know this, but lawyers are expensive. We don't have any more time to waste, so we'll send the bill directly to your parents."

Maybe I won't call her.

What would Dan Welch do?

Dear Business Affairs,

I received the Option Agreement for Sean Rosen's *A Week with Your Grandparents*. Please read it again. You obviously made a typing mistake. You accidentally wrote $500. You left out a few zeros.

Please make the correction and send it back to me as soon as possible.

Best,
Dan Welch

He didn't send this, of course. I actually *don't* think it was a typing mistake, because they wrote it out in both numbers and words: $500 (five hundred dollars).

I guess I could just go to Staples, buy some paper, come home, print out the Option Agreement, sign it, and get my $500 (five hundred dollars). I would still be in the movie business. A huge, famous entertainment company would still be paying me for my movie idea. I don't have to tell anyone how little they're paying me. Everyone will definitely think it's more. Much more.

But I can't. It doesn't feel right. I don't know what to do. I checked Dan Welch's e-mail, just in case business affairs wrote to him saying they made a mistake. They didn't. But there was an e-mail there.

To: Dan Welch Management
From: Dan Welch

Hey buddy,

Hows the managing? I was wondering, does anyone ever call you DW? Some of my friends do. One of em calls me DWI, but thats another story.

Hey I just put a rockin set of Cheerios bowls on ebay. Check it out if you want. Hope your havin a good one.

DW

No, DW. We're not "havin a good one."

I looked at the Cheerios bowls. They're pretty nice, but I don't eat Cheerios, and it would be weird to put another kind of cereal in those bowls.

I gave up and went to bed.

chapter 33

I woke up at 3:12 am. I can't stop thinking about the Option Agreement. It makes me kind of sick.

I started listening to science podcasts. The first one was about black holes, like in space, but I think it was for people who already know about them. I tried to follow it, but I couldn't. It's like when you put on Spanish radio and you don't speak Spanish. You listen for a while and you think somehow you're going to start understanding it. Every once in a while there's a word you know, but it just turns into random talking that plays in the background while you think about what you're trying not to think about.

Then I started listening to a podcast about insects, about how they reproduce. It was actually a little too interesting.

Finally I gave up trying to fall back to sleep. I got out of bed and looked out my window. All the houses were dark except for Mr. Bentley's. No one knows much about Mr. Bentley except he doesn't go to work and his lights are on most nights. Some people think he's some kind of genius. Maybe I should ring his doorbell right now and ask him to look at this Option Agreement.

I started looking around online. Some website said that for a movie option you can get paid anything from nothing to a million dollars. Five hundred dollars is a little better than nothing, but it's a lot worse than a million dollars. If they like it so much, and they want it so much, why would they pay me so little?

Sometimes doing things on your own is very, very lonely.

I went on Facebook. Nothing very interesting is happening to anybody. Brianna bought new jeans. My grandmother (Thorny Rosen) had a good colonoscopy, whatever that is.

I checked my e-mail. I don't know why. I hardly ever get e-mail. Sure enough, I didn't. But I saw the e-mail I got from Martin Manager. Since I started working with Dan Welch, I forgot about Martin. I read it again.

Dear Sean,

You certainly write a good letter. I admire your ambition and your confidence. I'm not going to represent you right now, but I'll be watching the trades to see how you do with _____ (my first-choice company, not the one I'm dealing with now).

As you proceed, if you have a specific business question I might be able to answer, try me.

Best,
Martin

I guess I do have a specific business question. WHAT THE BLEEP SHOULD I DO????

I sent this e-mail at 4:38 AM.

To: Martin Manager
From: Sean Rosen

Dear Martin,

I don't know if you remember, but I wrote to you about a month ago to see if you would possibly be my manager. I'm the 13-year-old. You said no (for now), but you said if I had a question I could ask you.

Here's my question. I had a meeting last week with Stefanie V. President (I used her real name, because he probably knows her), the Vice President of Production of _____ (her company). I told her an idea I have for a movie. She liked it. Today I got a 40-page Option Agreement from the business affairs department.

I know this company makes big, expensive movies, but

it sounds like they don't want to pay me very much. I know it's my first movie, but still.

I called Pastrami, Salami, Baloney & Hamm (I used their real name, too) and they said I would have to give them a 10,000 dollar retainer. I don't have 10,000 dollars.

I'm going to attach the Option Agreement just in case you want to look at it. You don't have to. Or you could just look at a few pages, not all 40.

I don't know what to do. I want them to make my movie, but what if it ends up making 100 million dollars? Some movies that aren't even very good make that much money. If I only get 7,500 dollars and it's my idea, I think I'll be very upset.

I'm afraid if I don't say yes right away they'll change their mind, and then I'll just be a seventh grader who was once almost in the movie business.

I know that managers usually make 15% of what the people they're managing earn. With this agreement, no matter what happens, I get 500 dollars. 15% of 500 dollars is only 75 dollars, but if you can help me with this, I'd be willing to pay you more than that.

Thanks for listening.

Sean

After I sent the e-mail I was able to go to sleep.

chapter 34

I woke up feeling better. I'm glad I wrote to Martin Manager, and I'm actually glad I have to go to school. Partly to take my mind off the stupid Option Agreement and partly because today is the President's Physical Fitness Test. My dad can't believe we still have this. He had to do it when he was in middle school.

This is my favorite day of the year in phys ed. I actually don't mind phys ed. I'm pretty good at certain games and sports. What I don't like is being on a team.

There's almost always something I don't like about my team. Sometimes it's a kid who hogs the ball. Sometimes it's a kid who doesn't want to play and doesn't even try. Either way, you lose when your team could have won. It's too frustrating.

The President's Physical Fitness Test doesn't have teams. Everyone just does the best they can in five different events—curl-ups (some people call them sit-ups), the shuttle run, the mile run, the V-sit reach, and pull-ups (some people call them chin-ups). You do it during your regular phys ed class.

You compete against all the kids your age in the country, and depending on your results, you can win different awards.

Participant Physical Fitness Award—if you're in the bottom 50% in any event

National Physical Fitness Award—if you're in the top 50% in every event

Presidential Physical Fitness Award—if you're in the top 15% in every event

They're all just certificates. You don't win a car or a week in Hawaii. Trust me, there are a lot of things in life where I'm in the bottom half, or even the bottom 15%. But not the President's Physical Fitness Test. It's something I'm actually good at.

I like all five events okay, but the one I'm the best at is pull-ups. For some strange reason I can do more pull-ups than anyone in my school. Some kids, including kids who look a lot stronger than me, can't even do one pull-up. If you can't do any pull-ups, you're allowed to do push-ups and you can still win a President's Award, but it's not exactly the same thing.

I don't practice pull-ups. The only time I ever do them is the day we take the President's test. I was walking by the gym the other day, and I went in and looked up at the bar.

It looks a little lower than it used to. Or maybe I got taller. Well, I did. Definitely. But I never thought it would matter for pull-ups. I never actually think about pull-ups. I just know I can do them. Or at least I could a year ago.

I also weigh more than I did last year. I'm not fat, but . . . Am I going to be able to pull up all that extra me with *these* arms? The bar may look lower, but it's still high.

I have to try it. I put down my knapsack and took off my sweatshirt. I had a T-shirt on underneath. I got a stool so I could reach the bar. I grabbed it. Yeah, I'm definitely heavier than last year.

I can't think about it. I have to start. Okay. Here . . . we . . . go. UNH!!! (Not out loud, but that feeling.) Your arms slowly start doing their job and you're coming up . . . up . . . and over. You made it! You're over the bar looking at the gym. Good work, Seany.

I only did three. I wanted to save myself for the test.

On the way to the gym today I ran into Brianna. She doesn't do the President's Physical Fitness Test. Her parents convinced the school to let her ballet classes count as phys ed.

"Sean, I can't believe you. You're really into this."

"I know."

"It's so funny."

"It is?"

"Yes. Did I tell you what happened at lunch?"

"No, but . . . I actually have to get going."

"Okay. Hope you win . . . or whatever."

I was in the locker room changing when I heard a familiar voice. "Look what's here." It was Doug talking about me to one of his football friends. "Rosen, what are *you* doing here? Today isn't the Yearbook Olympics."

They started changing. I wanted to move to another part of the locker room, but I made myself stay. And talk. "You guys aren't usually in this phys ed class."

His friend (Mike or Mac or Moose—I forget) said, "Some bozo stepped on Coach's stopwatch this morning, so some of us have to do the test now." I guess they call Mr. Obester "Coach."

I didn't have anything else to say, so I finished getting dressed, maybe a little faster than usual. I started to leave, but they were blocking me (possibly on purpose), so I went around the long way.

When the fitness test started, I stopped thinking about Doug. I got the V-sit reach over with. All you do is stretch. I don't know why it's part of a fitness test, but I'm good at it, so I don't care.

I always like the shuttle run. You run to a line, pick up a block, run back, and put the block down and then you do it all again. Really fast. Like in less than ten seconds. It reminds me of getting ready for school when I'm late. I'm always in the top 15 percent in the shuttle run.

The mile run is something we all do at the same time, and it's the only part of the fitness test we do outside. I got caught in a traffic jam of kids at the beginning, but as soon as there was room, I started running past a lot of people, including Doug. After I passed him he started running faster. I didn't look back, but I could hear him. It sounded like a herd of elephants. When a herd of elephants is chasing you, you run faster. Fortunately *my* faster is faster than Doug's, so after a little while, I didn't hear him anymore. It was my best mile ever.

Then it was sit-ups. For these, it's how many you can do without stopping. If you stop for more than three seconds, you're finished. I don't like doing sit-ups, but I don't mind them. The only problem with sit-ups is that you have to do them with a partner who holds your feet down. Mr. Obester said, "Okay, Sean and Doug." Oh, great.

Doug decided he would go first. Doug is bigger

than me. A lot bigger than me. My hands don't fit around his ankles. I tried to hold his feet down, but each time he did a sit-up I almost went flying across the gym. Doug got mad. "Coach! I need somebody else." Mr. Obester came over and held Doug's ankles and Doug started doing sit-ups.

I didn't really want Doug to hold my ankles, so I asked Ethan if he would do it. I started doing my sit-ups before Doug finished. Whoever holds your ankles counts out loud. If you're thirteen, you need fifty-three sit-ups to qualify for the President's Award. Doug did fifty-four. I did fifty-five.

Only the pull-ups were left. I asked Doug if he wanted to go first. He gave me a look that if it were translated into words would be words you're not supposed to say in school. He said, "No. *You* go."

I started doing pull-ups. People know I'm good at them, so everyone came over and counted my pull-ups together. "Fourteen . . . fifteen . . . sixteen . . ." You only have to do seven for the President's Award, but even though I grew, they're still easy for me, so I did twenty. The last one didn't count because my legs were kicking and you're not supposed to do that.

While I was on the pull-up bar, I saw Doug on the floor doing right-angle push-ups. That's what you do if you can't do pull-ups. I wasn't surprised. There's a lot of Doug to pull up.

There were four of us (including Javier) who qualified for a President's Physical Fitness Award. Doug didn't. I guess he got a National Fitness Award.

After it was over, I found Ethan. I don't know what kind of award he won. I didn't ask and he didn't tell me. We walked back to the locker room together. It felt like a good idea to be with someone even bigger than Doug. Just in case.

chapter 35

When I got home from school, I checked my e-mail. Martin Manager wrote back.

To: Sean Rosen

From: Martin Manager

Oh Sean, Sean, Sean . . . You're writing e-mails in the middle of the night.

I'm impressed that you managed to get an offer from a big studio. But that offer . . . I can only imagine how you feel, because I'm not an artist and I've never been assaulted the way you just were by being offered so little for something that is valuable.

Please don't take it personally. I know that's almost impossible, because it's your name on that contract, but believe me, they do this to everyone.

You would have no way of knowing this, but that was only their opening bid. Your idea is worth a lot more to them than what they offered you. They're hoping that since you don't have an agent and you don't have a manager (he doesn't know about Dan Welch) and you're only thirteen, you'll want to be in the movie business so badly (everybody does), that you'll agree to whatever outrageous conditions and miniscule payments they propose.

This deal can be dramatically improved, I promise you that. There's a part of me that would love to take them on and even try to punish them for trying to take advantage of a young boy.

I can't. I won't represent anyone under eighteen. I don't think kids should be in show business. It's a cruel world, and as a parent, I naturally want to protect kids from things that are bad for them. I'd leave the business myself, but my three kids are all in college.

Sean, even if you get a better deal, there are other things you need to think about. You'll be giving up your idea. They'll give it to a writer who will write the screen-play, and after that, they'll give it to another writer to rewrite the screenplay. Those writers will never speak to each other or to you.

Stefanie and her Directors of Development will be the ones giving orders to those writers. If the movie ever gets close to being made, people higher up in the com-pany will take over, and there will almost definitely be a new writer, someone who's already written a hit movie which may be nothing at all like *A Week with Your Grandparents*. At that point, no one who ever heard you talk about your idea will be involved with the proj-ect. Each new writer will try to make it his or her own thing.

If you're determined to do this, and I'd be surprised if you weren't, you can almost definitely find an agent or a manager to represent you now. You've done the hard work. You have a formal offer from a big studio. An agent or manager will be happy to get you a better deal and take their percentage. I can't promise they won't try to take advantage of you the way the studio tried to. I can promise you that whatever an agent or manager or studio executive tells you, they won't be able to protect your idea. They can't.

Good luck to you.

Best,
Martin

It always feels strange when an adult talks to you like you're also an adult. I mostly like it. I mean, it's better than when they act like you're not there, or that you're not able to understand what they're talking about.

But sometimes I wish they would treat me like a kid. It's easier being a kid. No one expects very much from you. People take care of you. All you really have to do is show up at school, do your homework, clean your room and try not to be a jerk.

I want to be in the entertainment business, doing things that grown-ups usually do, but I think I still want to be taken care of.

Is Martin Manager taking care of me by talking to me like an adult? Or is he telling me that if I want to work with adults, I can't be a kid anymore.

I don't know. I laid down on my bed. This time I didn't have any trouble crying.

chapter 36

There was a knock on my bedroom door. I closed it when I started crying. "Hey, Seany . . . can I come in?"

"I'm taking a nap."

"Sorry. Pizza tonight. Mom's working. What kind of ice cream do you want?"

"Chocolate. No. Let's try butter pecan. No. Dulce de leche."

"Final answer?"

"Dulce de leche."

"Got it."

Talking to my dad and thinking about ice cream made me feel better. I got out of bed and read Martin Manager's e-mail again. "You can almost definitely find an agent or a manager to represent you now."

I like that—someone to represent me. My representative. I would much rather be represented than managed.

But I can't have a new representative. It wouldn't be fair to Dan Welch. Without him, I never would have even thought of *A Week with Your Grandparents*. He's the one who got me the meeting at the studio. I don't know why a gigantic entertainment company is called a studio, but that's the word Martin used.

And if I got a new manager, what would I tell Stefanie and Brad? They know Dan. They like Dan. What would they think of me if I fired him?

Martin Manager said my deal could be dramatically improved. I wonder what he would ask the studio for if I was over eighteen and he was my representative.

I don't really understand what he said about all the different writers who would work on the movie. I'm the writer of *A Week with Your Grandparents*. I haven't actually written it yet, but I'm planning to.

When you look at the credits on a movie, a lot of times there's more than one writer. Sometimes there are four writers. Sometimes even more. I thought they all sat in a room and wrote it together. I didn't realize it's one, then another, then another, then another.

If the studio likes my idea enough to buy it, wouldn't they want me to write it? It's a story about kids, and I'm an actual kid. I know the story better than anyone else. They only heard it once. How will they even remember it all?

Unless they were recording our meeting, too. I wonder if they were.

I wonder if Stefanie knows that business affairs sent me this agreement. I wonder if she saw it.

I decided to let Dan Welch handle this.

To: Stefanie V. President
From: Dan Welch Management

Dear Stefanie,

You're probably a mom by now, and first of all, I want to congratulate you. As a parent myself, I can tell you that you'll never forget these first days with Marisa. I bet she's adorable.

I never knew Dan Welch has kids. I wonder how many. And how old they are. I can't fire him. He has a family.

I know you've been busy, so I'm sure you haven't seen the Option Agreement that your business affairs department sent me for Sean Rosen the other day. I'll attach a copy.

I'm actually not sure she didn't see the Option Agreement. I don't think Dan Welch is either, but he's smart to say it that way. If *I* was writing to her I would probably say, "Why? Why? Do you hate me?"

You and I don't really know each other, but this agreement doesn't seem like something you would ever send. Sean and I both like you so much, and you've certainly treated us well so far. Sean said you offered him water at your Skype meeting. Funny.

Just then I got a text from Buzz.

Be in hour bannd

I had no idea what he was saying. I texted him back.

Busy right now.

I got back to Dan's letter.

Sean thought you were seriously interested in *A Week with Your Grandparents*, and when I received your e-mail after the meeting, I thought so, too. For some reason, your business affairs department doesn't seem to think so.

Buzz texted again.

Not now rehurs 2sday

What is he talking about? I texted back.

What are you talking about?!

I should have just turned off my phone, but I didn't. I continued with Dan's letter.

As you know, *A Week with Your Grandparents* is a very good movie idea. Sean told me you asked him not to talk about it with anyone else. He hasn't, so far. But like most thirteen-year-olds, Sean can be a bit impatient.

I can't believe Dan said that about me. I think I'm actually *more* patient than a lot of kids. I know he only said it to make Stefanie a little nervous, but still. Buzz texted me again.

I told u a bannd

I went back over his other texts. Okay. He's asking me to be in his band. Buzz plays guitar. He's starting a band. But why ask *me*? I texted back.

I don't play anything.

He texted back right away.

Singger

Can he really not know how to spell singer? I actually do like to sing, and I think it would be really cool to sing with a band, but

a) I don't think I'm good enough

b) I really can't imagine singing in front of people.

I also couldn't imagine playing a character on stage before *Le Bistro* last year, but this sounds even harder to do. *Le Bistro* was so bad that *I* actually seemed good by comparison. But Buzz is good on the guitar and I'd be singing with him and whoever else is in the band. I texted: Who else is in the band?

He texted back.

Dug

He means Doug. Buzz was part of the whole tree house thing. I didn't know he stayed friends with Doug. I texted him.

Sorry. Can't. Too busy.

Where was I? Oh right. Dan Welch's e-mail to Stefanie.

I know this is the last thing you want to be thinking about right now, and if you can't help us with this, please let me know.

Best,
Sean

I guess I could try singing with the band for one rehearsal. If I don't sound good, I'll quit. And if I'm not comfortable being in a band with Doug, I'll quit. It sounds like I'm probably going to quit, so what's the point?

Good. I'm glad I figured that out, so I can stop wasting time thinking about the band, and get back to my movie. I read the letter over again.

To: Stefanie V. President
From: Dan Welch Management

Dear Stefanie,

You're probably a mom by now, and first of all, I want to congratulate you. As a parent myself, I can tell you that you'll never forget these first days with Marisa. I bet she's adorable.

I know you've been busy, so I'm sure you haven't seen the Option Agreement that your business affairs department sent me for Sean Rosen the other day. I'll attach a copy.

You and I don't really know each other, but this agreement doesn't seem like something you would ever send. Sean and I both like you so much, and you've certainly treated us well so far. Sean said you offered him water at your Skype meeting. Funny.

Sean thought you were seriously interested in *A Week with Your Grandparents*, and when I received your e-mail after the meeting, I thought so, too. For some reason, your business affairs department doesn't seem to think so.

As you know, *A Week with Your Grandparents* is a very good movie idea. Sean told me you asked him not to talk about it with anyone else. He hasn't, so far. But like most thirteen-year-olds, Sean can be a bit impatient.

I know this is the last thing you want to be thinking about right now, and if you can't help us with this, please let me know.

Best,
Sean

It sounds good, so I hit SEND. While the e-mail program was sending it, I could still see the bottom of the e-mail. OH NO!!! I signed it, "Best, *Sean*." It's from Dan.

I looked all over the screen for the cancel button. There *is* no cancel button.

Your message has been sent.

chapter 37

I am such an idiot. "Best, Sean." That's it. It's over. Why did Buzz have to text me?

It's not Buzz's fault. It's my fault. I was doing something really important and I stopped paying attention. I am such an idiot. I just threw away my whole career because I was busy imagining myself singing at the Grammys. I am such an idiot.

Stefanie is buying a big ad in *The Hollywood Reporter* right now.

THERE IS NO DAN WELCH.

DAN WELCH IS SEAN ROSEN.

AVOID THEM BOTH.

Why didn't I read it again before I sent it? I *did* read it again, but I was still thinking about the band. I used to read every word of Dan's e-mails over and over and over before sending them. We got too confident. No. *I* got too confident. There *is* no Dan Welch.

I wanted to blame the computer, I wanted to blame my phone, I wanted to blame Stefanie, but there's no one to blame except me. I got through dinner with my dad. I told him I wanted to watch the commercials so he wouldn't mute them. I didn't feel like talking. I didn't have any ice cream. I don't deserve ice cream.

I laid in bed for a long time, saying, "You are an idiot." At some point I fell asleep.

I woke up in the morning, and for about twenty seconds I forgot. I started to go to my computer to check Dan Welch's e-mail, but then I remembered "Best, Sean." I didn't even bother. Stefanie isn't going to write back to him now that she knows he doesn't exist. And I'm not in the mood for Collectibles Dan Welch.

I was in the kitchen eating cereal when my mom hurried in dressed in her uniform. She grabbed her lunch from the fridge, looked at me, and said,

"What's wrong?" She always knows.

"Nothing."

"I don't believe you." Fortunately she had to leave for work so she didn't have time to do a complete investigation.

School was awful. Thanks to my stupid mistake, I'll have to keep going. I had it all planned out. When we started shooting *A Week with Your Grandparents*, a tutor would come to my dressing room at the studio. I don't know why I thought writers get dressing rooms.

Or else I would share a tutor with the actors playing Chris and Chloe. We wouldn't be the same age, but the tutor would teach us all at the same time. It would be fun.

Or if I was too busy on the set every day, I would go to high school online. I've heard of some kids in show business who do that. That might be even better because you work at your own speed. Maybe I'd be able to do all four years of high school in four days. No. Four weeks. No. Four months. I don't know. It doesn't matter because my career is over, and I'm stuck going to school right here.

Realizing that was bad enough, but then at the end of the day we got our report cards. I couldn't believe what I was seeing. I got a C in French. That has to be a mistake.

I went to see Mademoiselle Fou. She was sitting on her desk texting. She didn't look up, even though I'm sure she heard me come in. She probably saw me too, but she acted like she didn't. Finally I said, "Excuse me . . . "

"En français, s'il te plaît." ("In French, please.")

I pointed to the C on my report card and said, *"Pourquoi?"* ("Why?") She looked at me for a second.

"Pourquoi pas?" ("Why not?")

I got mad. I switched back to English. "Come on. I got an A on every single test."

"Your grade is based both on tests and on class participation."

"What are you talking about? You never call on me!!!"

"That's not true, Gaston. I called on you and you couldn't perform the reading exercise."

"Marcel Proust?!! That's crazy! *You* couldn't

have read it either." I was about to say something else. Something worse. But instead I turned around and walked out of the classroom. She didn't come after me. She didn't have to. She won.

I was so mad I almost knocked over Matty, the custodian. I told him I was sorry and I just leaned against the wall for a minute to think.

Should I go back in there and tell her I'll do *Le Bistro* again? She would probably change my grade. Brianna would be happy.

No. I can't. I'll take the C.

Leaving school, I was in a daze. I've never actually gotten beaten up (thank goodness), but this is probably what it feels like.

French is bad, but the worst is wrecking my own career. I've been working so hard, and things actually seemed to be going pretty well.

It's true that nothing is happening yet with my big idea. But that was *my* decision. I never expected to start my career with a movie, but I actually loved working on it.

None of that matters now. My movie will never get made, and I'll never get to try out my big idea.

All because I wasn't paying attention. Because I was doing two things at once. Because one of the two things was way less important than the other, but I didn't act like it was.

When you get a text, you hear that sound, and you just drop whatever you're doing. Even if it's writing a letter to the Vice President of Production of a huge Hollywood studio asking her for more money for your movie. Maybe the "bannd" could have waited until Dan Welch finished what he was doing.

There were a lot of kids walking by, but I was just standing there. I couldn't stop saying mean things to myself. Then I heard someone say, "Hey, Sean."

I turned around. It was Ethan. I never heard him start a conversation before, but he picked a very good time. I thought about telling him what happened, since Ethan was almost Dan Welch and he's the only person not in Hollywood who knows about *A Week with Your Grandparents.* I couldn't. But I asked him if he wanted to go for a bike ride. We decided to meet back at school and we both went home to get our bikes.

chapter 38

My last bike got stolen. It was awful. You ride somewhere, you lock it up, then you come out and you go to where you left it, and it isn't there. Then you start wondering if you forgot where you left it. You know you didn't, but you start looking everywhere anyway. Then you finally face the fact. Someone stole it.

I loved that bike. It was a birthday present from my parents. I think it was really expensive. I need a bike because I ride all the time. My dad wanted to buy me the same bike again, but I wouldn't let him. I would always be afraid it would get stolen. So we went to the police bike auction.

I was sort of hoping they'd have my stolen bike,

but of course they didn't. The only bike that was the right size for me was a girl's bike. It wasn't pink or anything. It just didn't have that bar that goes between the seat and the handlebars.

I actually never rode a girl's bike before, so I tried it. It's a good bike. Not super nice, like my old bike, but I like the way it rides. And I found out it's actually easier getting on and off a girl's bike.

My dad said he could buy me a new bike, but I told him I liked this one. We got it for $23. Besides saving money, this bike has built-in robbery insurance. I don't know for sure, but I bet most bikes are stolen by boys, and the kind of boy who would steal a bike is the kind of boy who would never, ever ride a girl's bike. I don't have to worry about this bike.

Ethan was already at school when I got there. I was waiting to see if he was going to say something about me having a girl's bike. He didn't. We took a long ride around our town. Even though we didn't talk very much, it took my mind off everything bad that happened.

I had to pee, and we were pretty far away from my house. "Hey, Ethan . . . where do you live?" He told me the name of the street. It wasn't far. I asked if I could use his bathroom. We were near an alley between some buildings, and Ethan pointed and said, "You could just go over there."

I said, "Actually . . . I don't like doing things like that." He looked at me for a second. Ethan and I don't know each other very well, but I guess he figured out that he wasn't going to talk me into it, so he turned his bike around and said, "Follow me."

His house looks pretty much like mine, just a normal, not very big house. There was a car in the driveway. We went inside. It was kind of dark. I saw someone hurry out of the living room into the kitchen. I think it must have been his mom, but I couldn't really see her.

Ethan pointed me to the bathroom. I don't like to be nosy, but . . . Okay, I *do* sort of like to be nosy, but I try not to be too obvious about it. Looking around the house, and around the bathroom when the door was shut, I got kind of a weird feeling. I know Ethan's family moved to our town just a little while ago, but it looks like they never really moved in.

There aren't a lot of boxes around, but this house just doesn't look like a place where a family lives. They have chairs and tables and other furniture that families have, but nothing on the walls.

After I was done in the bathroom I saw a picture. It was a kid holding a trophy. I said to Ethan, "Is that you?" He said no, and he kind of hurried me out of the house. I never saw his mom or whoever ran out of the living room. Ethan got back on his bike, and I had to pedal fast to catch up to him.

We rode for a little while, then we stopped near that waterfall that isn't actually a waterfall. It was quiet for a while, just the sound of the water. I wanted to ask Ethan about his family, but I didn't know what question to ask.

I was still thinking about it when Ethan stood up. He got on his bike, said, "See you in school," then he rode off. I sat there for a few more minutes.

I was glad that neither of my parents was home.

My mom would have continued the questioning from this morning, and even my dad would have known I wasn't feeling very good. I'm not saying that my dad doesn't usually care how I feel. He does. But he never tries to talk me out of feeling bad. He knows people feel bad sometimes.

I grabbed a cookie and some pretzels and some lemonade and I went to my room. I tried to look at Facebook and I couldn't. I tried playing Ricochet Roulette and I couldn't. I don't know why, but I went back to my computer and looked at Dan Welch's e-mail account. He had a new e-mail.

To: Dan Welch Management
From: Stefanie V. President

OMG!!! Dan, I am so, so sorry. Thank you for contacting me. I swear to you on my infant daughter's extremely soft head, I did not see that contract. Please apologize to Sean. Ask him to pretend it didn't happen. Give me a couple of days, and business affairs will get back to you with something I'm sure you and Sean will be happy with. We don't want to lose him.

Gotta go. Marisa's hungry. Again. I can't even tell you.

By the way, it's hilarious that you signed your e-mail "Sean." I've been doing that a lot lately, too. I sign things with my husband's name, my mother's name, and just yesterday, "Esmeralda." She's the baby nurse.

But I recently expelled another human being from my body. What's your excuse?

♥ S

Dan's excuse is that Sean was busy imagining himself singing with a bannd in a stadium.

And guess what? That actually *was* a terrible deal they offered me. I guess Stefanie really *didn't* know before Dan told her.

I feel like I should write to Martin Manager to thank him for telling me I could get more. He was totally right. Unfortunately, I got the feeling from his e-mail that I shouldn't write to him again.

Stefanie actually thought it was funny that Dan signed his e-mail "Sean."

I can't believe it. I'm relieved, but I don't exactly feel happy. More like dizzy.

I wonder if I just used up all my good luck for the rest of the year. Or the rest of my life.

Okay, what did I learn from all this?

I have no idea. It was a horrible nineteen hours. I still think I was an idiot for not paying attention to what I was doing, but I'm glad my career isn't over. I don't know what's going on with Ethan's family, but it made me think there are worse things in life than a movie not getting made. But I'm really glad my movie *is* getting made.

chapter 39

Thank goodness it's a long weekend and nothing is going to happen in the next few days. Business affairs is working on our new Option Agreement, but I'm sure I won't get it right away.

I think Dan Welch would tell me to take a break from thinking about the movie. But he knows me pretty well and knows I probably can't. So he'd say, "Okay, then stop thinking about the Option Agreement and start thinking about the story." I actually think that's a good idea, because when I ask myself questions about the characters, I don't always know the answers.

Like for example, I don't know Chris and Chloe's parents' names. When they're in the middle of nowhere together in Bolivia, they have to call each other something. I wonder if they use each other's real names or if they're the kind of parents who call each other Honey or Pumpkin.

Chloe and Chris's mom wouldn't let anyone call her Pumpkin, even her husband. She likes people to use her real name, which is . . . Jill. It's a good thing she's not married to my dad, for two reasons. First of all, my dad doesn't call *anyone* by their real name. His three best friends are Turch, LeDuke, and Foul Shot.

The second reason is my dad's name is Jack. I don't like movies where the characters' names are a joke, like Jack and Jill. If you want it to feel real, they have to have real names. Chris and Chloe's dad's name is Steve.

I want this movie to feel like something that could actually happen. I know that grandfathers don't invent virtual reality time machines every day, but I believe that Chris and Chloe's grandfather did. And maybe your grandparents actually *are* way more interesting than you ever thought they were.

That makes me think about my grandparents. I don't know anything about my mom's father. Maybe he invented something. I'm going to ask Mary Lou, Mom's mother, when I see her this weekend. Maybe *she* invented something.

I got back to thinking about the movie. Sometimes when I'm thinking hard, it looks like I'm staring at whatever is right in front of me, but I'm not. My eyes are open and my head is pointed in that direction, but my brain is looking at whatever I'm thinking about.

Like right now, I'm facing one of those posters I'm going to take down before my next Skype meeting, but what I'm seeing is the house where Jill, Steve, Chris, and Chloe live. It's bigger and more modern than ours. So when Chris and Chloe go to their grandparents' house, it feels very old-fashioned to them.

Then there's Chris's cheerleader girlfriend, Sabrina (thank you, Ethan). During the whole week with his grandparents, Sabrina is constantly calling and texting Chris. He used to like that, but now he notices the things she talks about. When you're away from home, nothing at your school sounds very important.

Part of it is that Chris has been spending a lot of time with his grandmother, who always wants to help mankind. He can't imagine Sabrina doing that unless it might help her get into a good college or get her picture in the paper. It makes him think.

What about Chloe? What happens on her other trips to the past?

Back at home, Chloe is frustrated because she's twelve, and her mom still treats her like a little girl. She can't go to the mall with her friends unless a parent is with them the whole time. Worst of all, Chloe isn't allowed to be on Facebook. You're supposed to be thirteen, but every one of Chloe's friends has an account. Chloe wants to go back in time to see what her mom was like when *she* was twelve. But her mom isn't there to spit on the slide.

Chris, who's pretty good at science, says, "Aren't there other ways to get Mom's DNA? She kissed us good-bye. Maybe some of her DNA is still on our faces."

"Wait!" Chloe runs upstairs and gets her hat. Her mom borrowed it last winter and Chloe finally took it back because her mom didn't need it in Bolivia. She pulls a hair from the hat and hands it to Grandpa. "This one is definitely Mom's. I don't have those roots."

Grandpa isn't sure the machine will work with hair because he always used spit, but he'll try. He sets the machine for the date of Chloe's mom's twelfth birthday.

Chloe climbs into the machine. We see what she sees, which is very blurry, and we hear what she hears, which sounds like people talking under water. It's because the machine isn't used to working with hair. Outside, Grandpa is turning knobs and pushing buttons. Finally the green lights come on.

Inside, everything is now clear. Chloe is at a multiplex, which is show-business language for a movie theater that shows a lot of different movies. Every movie theater is like that now, but in 1983, only some movie theaters were multiplexes. I looked it up.

Chloe sees a bunch of twelve-year-old girls she doesn't recognize, and a woman who looks kind of familiar. It's Jill's mom, Chloe's other grandmother. She's taking the girls to the movies for Jill's birthday. Chloe can't figure out which girl is Jill, until one of them gets into an argument with Chloe's grandmother. That's Chloe's mom.

They were planning to see *Flashdance*. Jill is dressed like the girl in the *Flashdance* poster, with her hair all curly and the sweatshirt with one bare shoulder sticking out. Jill's mom keeps pulling the sweatshirt up and Jill keeps pulling it down.

They're arguing about *Flashdance*.

"Mom, you said we could."

"You forgot to mention it's rated R."

"I didn't know. I swear. Anyway, it's fine. We're here with you. You're an adult."

"It is *not* fine. Even if I thought it was okay for you, which I don't, I still have to call each of these girls' parents."

"No, you don't."

"Yes. I do. And if even one of them says no . . ."

"Mom . . ."

"I don't think I have enough change to make all those calls." (This was before everyone had cell phones.)

"Okay, forget *Flashdance*. We'll see *Risky Business*."

"No, we won't. That one's rated R, too. How about *Mr. Mom*. It's PG."

"As in Pretty Gross. Forget it. Thanks for wrecking my birthday, Mom."

Suddenly it's over. Chloe's grandmother pushed the red button. Chloe can't wait for her mom to get back from Bolivia so she can find out what happened that day. She'll remind her mom what it's like to be a twelve-year-old girl who wants to be treated like a grown-up.

Okay. I made some progress. I can start packing for our family trip tomorrow. We're leaving early.

chapter 40

Once a year we visit my mom's family. They all live near each other, so they get together a lot, but when *we* come it's kind of a special occasion. We always go on a three-day weekend, like Presidents' Day or Columbus Day. We never go for Thanksgiving or Christmas. My mom says, "It's too loaded." When I ask her what it's loaded with, she just shakes her head and says, "Everything."

I decided to show my mom and dad my report card on the way to see my cousins. My parents like when I get good grades, but sometimes I don't, and they don't yell at me or anything. When they saw the C in French, they weren't mad, but they were surprised.

I always get an A in French. They've heard me speak French. They came to *Le Bistro* last year. Mademoiselle Fou was all over them, telling them what a little Maurice Chevalier I am. I actually like Maurice Chevalier. I saw him on YouTube, but I'm not really like him.

I told my parents I got A's on all the tests. I also told them that I'm not going to be in *Le Bistro* this year. My dad said, "Hence the C." My dad usually talks like someone who never went to college, but every once in a while something slips out.

They asked what I want to do about this. They said they could come in and talk to Mademoiselle Fou. Trust me, my parents are not the ones who are always at school yelling at teachers. I told them I'll think about it.

Anyway, my mom has two brothers and three sisters, and each one has at least three kids. We actually *need* a three-day weekend just to see everyone. The first two nights we stay with Uncle John and his family. He's not my mom's favorite or anything, but he has the biggest house and my parents can have their own room.

I share my cousin Declan's room. Declan is twelve and he's on like a million teams. His room is filled with equipment and sports posters and trophies. It's kind of interesting for both of us because he doesn't have any friends like me and I don't have any friends like him.

He has bunk beds. I'm not sure why one kid needs two beds, but it comes in handy when we visit. I always get the top bunk, because Declan is scared of heights. It actually isn't that high, but if you're scared of something, someone telling you why you shouldn't be doesn't really change anything.

After two nights at Declan's house, we always have to spend one night at Aunt Kathleen's house. She gets jealous. She's the one with five kids and a dog and two cats.

I like going to Aunt Kathleen's because I like the animals. Even though they haven't seen me for a year, I think Rex and Spice and Elvis remember me. Or else they don't remember me, but for some reason they like me. It makes me wish my mom was a dog person or my dad was a cat person or both.

Aunt Kathleen and Uncle Peter's house is a little small for how many people and animals live there. So on the night we stay there, my mom, my dad, and I all sleep in the basement in the playroom. They sleep on a couch that turns into a bed, and I sleep on an air mattress on the floor.

I like my parents a lot. In fact, I love them. But I don't actually want to be roommates with them. I wasn't one of those kids who always climbed into bed with his parents, and even if I was, I'm thirteen now.

Every year before we leave on this trip, my dad says, "Why don't we just stay at the Holiday Inn? We'll be with them from right after we wake up until right before we go to sleep. Isn't that enough?" Not for my mom's family, it isn't.

It's fun for a few days. At home, there's only one kid and no animals, so even when all three of us are in the house, you hardly hear a sound. When we visit my mom's family, it's never quiet. And this year, it took my mind off waiting for the new Option Agreement.

It was also good because I could do some

research for the movie. My mom's mom is nothing at all like Thorny Rosen or like Chloe and Chris's grandmother in the movie. She never tells you the right thing to do. She's Mary Lou, and if you call her Grandma or Nana or Mimi or Grammie, she doesn't answer. I guess she had enough of being a mom after six kids, so now she acts like she's a friend of the family instead of the grandmother.

Here are some of the questions I asked my cousins about their other grandparents:

1. Do your parents ever leave you alone with your grandparents?
2. What do you do with your grandparents when you're together?
3. How do you picture your grandmother and your grandfather when they were your age?
4. If you could ask your grandparents any question about your mom or dad, what would you ask them?

I experimented with talking to them one at a time and doing group interviews with the brothers and sisters of the same family. It actually worked well both ways. People like to be interviewed. Especially if you're holding a cool-looking digital voice recorder.

It was a good weekend, except for a few fights. There are always a few fights. It's never the kids. It's always my mom's sisters and brothers and their husbands and wives, and it's always after nine at night.

The adults start drinking about five o'clock, and for the first hour or two, it's fun. They're in a good mood, joking around, talking to you more than they did all day. But by nine, some of the ones who keep drinking start to get a little mean, and that's when the fights happen.

My mom never fights with anyone, but some-times my dad tries to stop a fight, and then he's in the fight. People don't hit each other (except once), but it's still a fight. Everyone who fought says they're sorry by the end of the weekend, and on the way home my mom says, "Just be glad it wasn't Christmas."

chapter 41

While we were away, Dan Welch got a Revised Option Agreement from business affairs. They didn't apologize for the first one they sent. They didn't say anything about what Martin Manager called "the outrageous conditions and miniscule payments" they offered me the last time. They just sent another document. This one is *fifty* pages.

I tried to figure out what's different. At first it looked like they only changed some of the numbers, but then I saw what they added. It's big. Now if the studio makes *A Week with Your Grandparents,* I get some of the net profits.

I'm so excited. Stefanie must have really

yelled at them. I'm actually a part of it now. If the studio makes money, I make money. It's only 1 percent of the net profits, but 1 percent of a million dollars is 10,000 dollars. 1 percent of 100 million dollars is a million dollars. And 1 percent of a billion dollars is 10 million dollars.

I know I'm probably not going to make 10 million dollars. First of all, my movie might not make a billion dollars (like *Shrek* or *Toy Story* or *Pirates of the Caribbean*). Second of all, they have to pay to make the movie and to advertise it. So even if it does make a billion dollars, that won't all be net profit. I don't actually know what net profit is. The ten extra pages of the Revised Option Agreement are the Net Profit Definition. I haven't even tried to read that part.

The other numbers are a lot better, too. Instead of paying me 500 dollars for the option, now they're going to pay me 10,000 dollars. And if they "purchase the property" they have to pay me 50,000 dollars (minus the 10,000 they already paid me). That's a whole lot more than 7,500 dollars. But I think the biggest thing is that I get a share of the profits.

What will I do with 10,000 dollars? There isn't anything I want to buy right now, but I do want to celebrate. I got on my bike and rode over to Baskin-Robbins and bought myself an ice cream cone. Jamoca Almond Fudge. Sometimes I get it when I'm happy about something and sometimes I get it when I'm sad about something. It always makes me feel good. I like buying it with my own money.

When I got home, that giant Revised Option Agreement was waiting for me. I'm not sure what to do. Should I just sign it? Should I try to read it and understand what it says? Should I hire a lawyer? Should I try to get an agent?

Dan Welch actually did a very good job for me, especially after Martin Manager told us we could get more than what they offered us at first. I wish I could send the Revised Option Agreement to Martin.

I read his last e-mail again. One part of it confuses me.

You'll be giving up your idea. They'll give it to a writer who will write the screenplay, and after that, they'll give it to another writer to rewrite the screenplay. Those writers will never speak to each other or to you.

I don't want to give up my idea. I don't want them to give it to a writer. I want *me* to be the writer. I *am* the writer.

Maybe Martin is wrong. I started reading the Revised Option Agreement to see if it says anything about using other writers.

I had to stop for dinner. The second I sat down, my mom said, "Okay, what is it?"

"What is what?"

"You look overwhelmed. Did the president ask you to fix the budget deficit?"

She's so good it's scary sometimes. I'm surprised she didn't invite Dan Welch to dinner.

"Mom . . . Don't you watch the news? I already fixed the budget deficit."

She smiled like that was a little funny, then she kept looking at me like, "Okay. Don't tell me. But sooner or later I'm gonna find out."

After dinner I went up to my room and got back to the Revised Option Agreement. Trying to understand all these words I never heard of, I got an idea for an invention. You know how on your computer you can translate something from French or Russian or Japanese into English in like two seconds?

My invention, or actually my idea for an invention, is something that can translate the way lawyers talk, like in my Option Agreement, into English. I don't see why that wouldn't work.

This idea isn't like my big entertainment idea, because I don't care if someone steals it. In fact, I hope you do. Forget stealing. I'm *giving* you this idea. You can have all the money from the Agreement Translator. Just invent it really soon and give me a free one.

I keep trying to read this thing, and I keep falling asleep. I got a text from Brianna.

I'm bored. ☹

I texted back. **I'm sleepy.**

B: Thanks. Now I'm bored and sleepy.

S: Go to sleep.

B: No.

S: Go shopping.

B: I hate shopping online. It never fits. It never looks like the picture. You have to wait for it, then you have to send it back.

S: Now we're both bored.

B: You're the one who brought up shopping.

S: You're right as usual. Gotta go. C u tomorrow.

Brianna is one of the few people (other than me) who uses punctuation when they text.

I spent another half hour going through the Option Agreement. They're still going to own all rights to the plot, theme, title, characters, sequels, and everything else anyone will ever think of in perpetuity throughout the universe. But I don't see anything in here about who is actually going to write the movie.

I could spend my whole 10,000 dollars hiring Pastrami, Salami, Baloney & Hamm, but I don't want to. Dan Welch has to write to Stefanie again. I turned off my phone so I won't get any texts about bannds.

To: Stefanie V. President
From: Dan Welch Management

Hi Stefanie,

Thanks for the immediate action on Sean Rosen's Option Agreement. It's much better now. I like the way you work.

I've only taken a quick look, and sorry if I missed something obvious, but I don't see anything in here about Sean writing *A Week with Your Grandparents*.

I assume you want him to write it, because I can't imagine anyone who could do a better job on this than Sean. He's been working on it since your meeting, and he's excited to tell you the new parts. I'm sure you'll like it.

Please ask your business affairs department to revise

the Revised Option Agreement so it's clear that Sean will be writing the movie. If that's already in the agreement, please tell us where we can find it.

How's Marisa?

Best,
Dan

Before sending it, I checked about fifty times to make sure I signed it "Dan" and not "Sean."

like letting Dan Welch handle the business stuff. I'm much better at the creative parts. I have my list of directors ready for Stefanie. I started a list of actors, too. The parents and the grandparents should be famous movie stars, but I think Chris and Chloe should be played by actors we don't know yet. You'll meet them for the first time in *A Week with Your Grandparents*. I'll be glad when the agreement is signed, so Stefanie and I can really get to work.

I got to school early today and went to the principal's office. Trish, his secretary, likes when I stop by. I came to see if I can switch from French to Spanish. They usually don't let people do that in the middle of a school year.

I decided not to talk about Mademoiselle Fou. I told Trish that I really love foreign languages (which I do), and I plan to travel a lot (which I do). I want to be able to talk more to Javier's family, and I want to be able to translate what I write into different languages (*Une Semaine avec Votre Grandsparents, Una Semana con Sus Abuelos*). About 400 million people in the world speak Spanish and only about 100 million people in the world speak French. Spanish would be four times more useful.

Trish thinks she'll be able to do it. That would be so great. I'm actually proud of myself for taking care of a big problem without dragging my parents in.

Then, unfortunately, I had to go to the bathroom. I don't know if you've ever been in a middle school boys' room. It's not somewhere you'd ever want to go unless you absolutely had to. I'm not a clean freak, not even close, but that room is gross.

Sometimes you have no choice. This was one of those times. I was standing there holding my nose, doing my business. I heard the door open and it suddenly got a little darker. Not like someone turning off the light, but like something big *blocking* the light. Like an eclipse. I thought maybe it was Ethan.

Then I heard, "Look what's here." I was looking straight ahead. When I turned, standing next to me, doing *his* business, was Doug. If I could have, I would have walked away, but once you start it's hard to stop.

Doug said, "I hear you're not gonna be in the band." I know that some people actually enjoy talking while they go to the bathroom, but I'm not one of them. I didn't say anything. Doug said, "That was Buzz's idea, not mine."

I finished, finally. I thought about leaving without washing my hands. Some people do that. While I was deciding, Doug said, "Don't go anywhere. I have to talk to you."

I washed my hands and waited. Doug finished (didn't flush, didn't wash) and came over to me. "I know all about your agent."

What?! NO!!!!! This can't be happening. Not now. Buzz!! You *told* him?

"I don't have an agent." I actually don't. Dan Welch is my manager.

"Don't lie to me. He helped you sell some movie or something."

This is officially a nightmare. I was sure Buzz would forget that whole conversation. Why did I have to tell him? What's Doug going to do? Will he tell the studio that *I'm* actually Dan Welch?

"Are you rich now?"

I laughed. "Do I look like I'm rich?"

"No. You look like the same little loser you always were. Anyway, I want his number."

This is terrible. Stay calm. Stay calm. "Whose number?"

"Your agent. What's his name . . . Dave Motts. What the hell are you laughing at?"

"I'm not." (I was.) I told Buzz it was Welch like the grape juice, but he must have told Doug it was Motts like the apple juice. And that his name was Dave, not Dan.

"I don't even have a phone number for him. Why do you want to talk to him?"

"Our band, you idiot. If he can make *you* famous . . . "

"Doug. Do you actually think I'm famous?" He

didn't say anything. "Here's what I can do. When your band records something, I promise I'll get Dave Motts to listen to it. If he likes it, I'm sure he'll want to represent you."

Doug left the boys room, then I left. That wasn't so bad.

You know . . . Dan Welch actually *could* represent other people. Maybe not Buzz and Doug's band, but other really good people who can't get an agent. It's an interesting idea.

Walking home from school I passed Mr. Bentley's house. He was in his front yard, standing on a ladder near a tree, holding a long orange extension cord with nothing plugged into it.

I stood there and watched him for a minute. I don't think he saw me. He was concentrating really hard. Suddenly he threw the extension cord up into the tree. I don't know what he was trying to do, but the extension cord came back down and hit him on the head and he almost fell off the ladder.

I ran over. He looked a little embarrassed. I said, "I can hold the ladder if you want."

"Who are you?"

"I'm Sean. Your neighbor. I live right over there." I pointed to our house.

"Oh, the plumber's kid."

"Right. What are you trying to do?"

He pointed up. "See that big branch? I'm pretty sure it's dead. I'm trying to throw the extension cord so it goes over the branch, and then I'll pull it down."

"With the extension cord?"

"I've done it before. You know how much these tree guys get?"

"Actually, no." But now I was curious. "How much?"

"It's highway robbery."

I still don't know how much the tree guys get, but I held the ladder while Mr. Bentley threw the extension cord. He kept missing, and the fourth time it landed on me. The plug part actually hurt.

"One more try, then I have to get started on my homework." This time the extension cord went over the branch. Mr. Bentley came down off the ladder, grabbed both ends of the extension cord and started pulling. I thought about offering to help, but it looked like if the branch broke off, it would hurt a lot more than the extension cord when it hit you in the head.

He was still tugging when I left. Maybe Mr. Bentley isn't a genius.

I grabbed some cookies, and for good luck, some grape juice, and I went upstairs to check Dan Welch's e-mail.

To: Dan Welch Management
From: Stefanie V. President

Dan,

I got your e-mail. Call me at 555-666-7777 (not her real number). It's my cell. Call anytime. I never sleep anymore.

S

I tried very hard to stay calm. Then I yelled the word "NO!!!!!!!!" really loud. Fortunately, no one else was home. But Mrs. Mancino, our next door neighbor, heard me. She called to see if everything was all right. I told her I was just about to break my record on Halo when my Xbox crashed. I actually don't have an Xbox. And she probably saw me outside a minute ago helping Mr. Bentley. Whatever.

What does Stefanie want to talk about? I'm going to write this movie. Why can't she just say that? Why can't she put it in an e-mail? What's with the phone all of a sudden?

Dan Welch is not going to call her. He *can't* call her. What can he do?

Dear Stefanie,

Great to hear from you. I would love to call you, but a bizarre series of accidents destroyed every one of the cell towers where I live. It's terrible. Fortunately, we still have electricity, so feel free to send me an e-mail.

No. If Dan has e-mail, he can call her on the internet.

Dear Stefanie,

Great to hear from you. I would love to call you, but unfortunately, I was born without a mouth. I usually don't tell people, but I know I can trust you and you won't hold it against me. If it's okay with you, we'll continue to "talk" by e-mail.

No.

Dear Stefanie,

Great to hear from you. I would love to be able to call

you, but unfortunately, I have a terrible cold and I completely lost my voice. We can wait until I'm better and
talk then.

The reason we might not want to do that is Sean. He
keeps asking me to call _____ (my first-choice
entertainment company) to talk about *A Week with
Your Grandparents.*

Why don't we stick to e-mail for now, and if we can't
work things out, I'll call you as soon as I can talk again.

Best,
Dan

P.S. We could also do an online chat. Just tell me when.

That's the one he actually sent. Of course I
read it twenty times first. That's one of the reasons
that Dan Welch having a chat with Stefanie makes
me nervous. There won't be time to make sure we
don't make any stupid mistakes.

I know how Dan writes an e-mail, but I don't

know how he chats. I never even thought about him chatting until he suggested it. I hope he knows what he's doing. I don't know why he mentioned a phone call when he's better, because he can't ever talk on the phone.

Why does she want to talk to him? He asked her a simple question. Maybe she's afraid that if I write the movie, we're going to ask for more money or a bigger share of the profits. Actually, that would be fair, but the main thing is I want it to come out right.

The way Stefanie told Dan to call her sounded like an emergency. Like, "We have to talk right away." Why?

I've heard of anxiety attacks. I wonder if I'm having one right now. If I am, I wonder how you make it stop.

I was looking up anxiety attacks when my phone beeped. It was a text. I was afraid to look. It doesn't make sense, but I thought it was Stefanie sending a text to Dan Welch. Like maybe I gave her my phone number by mistake.

I was scared, but I made myself look.

Wottup

It's Buzz. Maybe it's Buzz trying to sound like a hip hop guy or maybe it's Buzz not being able to spell, but it's Buzz. I texted back.

Not much. You?

I know. How can I say "Not much" in the middle of a possible anxiety attack. But if I tried to explain what was up it would be the world's longest text, and then Buzz would just tell it all to Doug and whoever they got to sing in their bannd.

Anyway, when people say "Wottup" or "What's up? or "How are you?" most of the time they don't actually want to know. Buzz texted again.

Chilin U

Why did he say "U"? I just told him what I'm doing. "Not much." It isn't true, but I told him. I understand not reading all the way to the end of a long, boring e-mail, but I think people do that with texts, too. You get the main idea, then you stop reading it, even if the whole text is three words long.

Buzz is saying let's hang out, and part of me

wants to, but I know I can't stop thinking about all this.

Can't. Homework.

It's a good thing I didn't go to Buzz's, because a few minutes later, I heard a sound from my computer. I left Dan Welch's e-mail account open. It was Stefanie, starting a chat.

STEFANIE: Hi Dan. Are you there?

Damn. I wanted more time to think about what Dan is going to say before he has to actually say it. He can just not answer her. Maybe he's away from his computer and his other devices. Maybe he's in the bathroom. I wonder if Dan Welch is one of those people who bring their devices with them to the bathroom.

I don't know what to do. If I don't answer, I'll just worry about what Stefanie wants to say. I want it to be over with, but I don't want to mess it up. If I wait until tomorrow, I still won't know what to do.

We might as well do it right now. She's the one

who wants to talk to him, so maybe he can mostly listen. I trust Dan Welch.

DAN: Yes, I'm here. How are you? How's Marisa?
STEFANIE: Sleep deprived, upset stomach, crying a lot.
That's me. She's fine.
DAN: My wife went through that, too. She's okay now.
STEFANIE: How old is your youngest?

How should I know? Why did he have to bring up his family?

DAN: 13.
STEFANIE: It better not take me 13 years to recover from this. So you have experience with kids Sean's age.
DAN: Yes. I do.
STEFANIE: Obviously he can't write the screenplay.

I'm glad this isn't a Skype meeting, because the second I read that, I almost started crying. Then a second later I got so mad I punched something. My bed, actually.

I came back to the computer.

DAN: Why not?

STEFANIE: He's 13. He's never written a screenplay (Has he?). Even if he was 24, we'd bring in a name screenwriter to write it. You know how it works.

I do? He does? That makes no sense to me. What's a name screenwriter? I have a name. Anyway, all those name screenwriters, whoever they are, were once people who never wrote a screenplay.

DAN: I think Sean can do it.

STEFANIE: Dan, he's absolutely adorable, and I saw his podcast. Very cute. But we're talking about a big Hollywood feature film. I couldn't write it. You couldn't write it. We'll get someone who can.

What does she mean, she saw my podcast? Which one? "Very cute"? I bet she didn't even watch a whole one.

DAN: How about letting him try it, and if you're not happy with it, you can bring in someone else.

STEFANIE: Even if I could convince the studio to do that, which I absolutely can't, we don't have the time or money to wait around for something I know right now we'll never be able to use.

How can you say that?! I never had a movie idea until a few weeks ago, but I thought of one in a day that you like enough to pay me 10,000 or 50,000 or a million dollars for. And what do you mean, you don't have the time? The Option Agreement gives you five years!

DAN: I'm not sure what to do.
STEFANIE: Tell Sean he can't write it.

Dan didn't know what to say. No one said anything for a little while.

STEFANIE: Tell Sean that _____ (my first-choice entertainment company) won't let him write it either.

Is that really true?

More time went by.

STEFANIE: No one will.

DAN: I think he can do it.

STEFANIE: You're a loyal manager, Dan. Sorry. Let us know whether or not Sean wants this to happen. Gotta go. You-know-who is crying. I might need a pep talk from your wife.

STEFANIE: Oh. I forgot. One more thing. Business affairs didn't know Sean is only 13. Since he's a minor, one of his parents will have to sign the contract. They'll send you a new signature page tomorrow. Talk to you when your voice comes back.

chapter 44

It's almost dark, but I have to get out of my house. I got on my bike. My parents don't really like me riding my bike when it's dark. My bike has a light but it's broken, so I took a flashlight with me. I left a note.

OUT. BACK SOON.

I rode over to the tree house. I climbed up and just sat there for a few minutes. Last time I brought pillows so I would be comfortable. This time I didn't. I'm not comfortable. I don't want to be comfortable. There's nothing to be comfortable about.

Why is life like this? You think things are good, and then suddenly they're bad. Like the last time I was up here. I was sure there was good news in that envelope, not a stupid letter telling me that whatever my idea was, they already have it.

I guess *A Week with Your Grandparents* was one idea they didn't already have. Now they want it, but they don't want *me*. I still don't get why they won't even let me *try* to write it.

Was Stefanie just being nice to me because she wants the idea? How much is it worth? I knew it wasn't $500. Is it $10,000? Is it $50,000? Is it $50,000 and 1 percent of the net profits? Is it a lot more? I don't know.

So I'll have some money, and they'll give my idea to a "name screenwriter." Maybe it will even be someone who wrote a movie I like.

But this is a new movie. This is *A Week with Your Grandparents*. How can anyone, even a name screenwriter, write this movie without talking to me?

What if I end up hating the movie? What if they make Chloe one of those sarcastic girls, where everything she says is a mean joke? What if they make Chris a dumb jock? What if Steve and Jill, their parents, are horrible selfish people who only think about work and actually don't care about their kids?

What if the grandparents are like stupid movie grandparents, where Grandpa is a crazy scientist who farts all the time and Grandma is a little old lady who always talks about sex? What if all those awful people suddenly turn into perfect people right at the end of the movie?

That could happen. *A Week with Your Grandparents* could turn into a movie that I would actually hate. I'll have 50,000 dollars and 1 percent of the net profits, but when we drive past a movie theater that has YOUR GRANDPARENTS on the sign, I won't feel proud. I'll duck down in the back seat so I don't have to see it. And so nobody sees *me*, the kid who made you waste your money going to see a stupid bad movie.

I just heard a siren. From where I am in the tree, I can see an ambulance go by with its lights flashing. This tree isn't in the middle of a forest. It's in an empty lot a few blocks from the main street in my town.

I wonder who's in the ambulance. Mr. Bentley? Maybe my mom will help take care of him. She's working tonight.

If I sell my idea, and the movie turns out really bad, at least no one will know I had anything to do with it. No one except Ethan, and he won't tell anyone.

Wait a minute. Sometimes near the beginning of movies you'll see "Story by So and So." I definitely don't want it to say "Story by Sean Rosen" if the movie sucks. I wonder if it has to say that. I might have to read that stupid Revised Option Agreement again. And what's this garbage about me being a minor? If I'm old enough to have something you want, I'm old enough to sign my own contract.

Maybe Dan Welch can sign the Revised Option Agreement. He has a wife and kids. His youngest is my age. He's not a minor.

What would my parents say about this? Would they feel bad that I did it all without telling them? Would their feelings be hurt that I trusted Dan Welch, but I didn't trust them?

It isn't that I don't trust them. This just isn't something they know about. My dad is still mad at that "producer" he introduced me to. He probably thinks everyone in the business is like that guy. Maybe they are.

My mom would be afraid I'll get my feelings hurt. Maybe I will.

Sitting up in the tree I feel very, very small. Even smaller than I was when I used to come here with Buzz and Doug. I feel like a tiny little molecule.

Knowing that Stefanie and the business affairs department of a huge company have been talking about this little molecule and writing fifty-page contracts for him and offering him thousands of dollars and part of their profits should make me feel bigger, but it doesn't. Am I being piggy for wanting even more than that?

It's really quiet now. All you can hear is the leaves when the wind blows. It's the perfect temperature. I love nights like this. Why do I feel so sad?

I think I have to do this. I think I have to

sell them my idea. I think I have to do it for the money. I know how much my parents earn. I probably shouldn't have, but I looked at their income tax forms.

They're a plumber and a nurse. I'm not saying we're poor. We're not. We have a house and a car and a van. Everything's fine, but in a few years I'm going to start college.

Some colleges cost more than 50,000 dollars each year, and college is four years. I don't have to go to one of those super expensive colleges, but even one that costs half as much, or even less than half as much is still going to be very expensive for my family.

If I can chip in 10,000 or 50,000 dollars from selling my movie idea, that will help a lot.

Anyway, *A Week with Your Grandparents* is just one idea. I can come up with other movie ideas. Maybe not in a day, and maybe they won't be as good as this one, but maybe they will.

And remember, this isn't even my big idea. It's just something I thought of during my trial run. Maybe Dan Welch can help me sell my big entertainment idea to the gigantic company that I actually *do* want to work with. I know Stefanie said the other company won't let me write my own movie either, but maybe she was wrong. Anyway, my big entertainment idea isn't even a movie.

I was starting to feel a tiny bit better, so I came down from the tree, got on my bike, turned on the flashlight, and rode home.

chapter 45

When I got home, my dad was there. He was waiting for me to get home before going to get our pizza. I asked if we could eat at the kitchen table instead of in front of the TV. I think maybe it's time to talk to my dad about what's happening. He said, "Wherever you say, Seany."

I usually don't drive to the pizza place with him, but for some reason I wanted to. In the van I asked my dad about college.

"College? You know, classes, parties, being away from home. You're gonna love it."

"Did *you* love it?"

"Yeah. For a while." No one said anything for a

minute. "You probably want to know why I stopped loving it."

"I do, actually."

"Well, Seany . . . I was in college when my father got nailed."

"Nailed?"

"Arrested. They came to his office one day and took him away. He was a crook, Seany. He stole money from a bunch of people who trusted him."

I didn't know what to say. I sort of knew it was something like that, but hearing my dad actually say it, it was worse than I thought.

We got to the pizza place.

"You coming inside?"

"Nah." I sat in the van and thought about my dad in college. I wonder if he was in a class or at a party or just in his dorm room when he found out about his father.

Dad came back with the pizza and we drove home. "Seany, listen to me. It's not genetic. My grandfather was an honest guy, and I'm an honest guy and you're an honest guy."

I felt a little sick when he said that. When he finds out about Dan Welch, will he still think I'm an honest guy?

"What did you do when you found out about your dad?"

"Stupid stuff. I got drunk a lot. I stopped going to classes. I didn't tell anyone, but I didn't have to tell anyone. It was all over the news. I wouldn't talk to my mother, because I was sure she was in on it. She wasn't. I mean, maybe she should have asked him where all the money was coming from, but everyone just thought he was really good at what he did.

"I dropped out of college. After I found out it was being paid for with money he stole, I couldn't do it anymore. I got a job in construction, which I liked. I guess I could have gone back to school, but my father had all kinds of college degrees and he turned out to be a jerk, so I decided to train as a plumber."

After a minute he said, "But that was *me*. You're going to college."

I said, "Yeah, I actually want to go to college."

"Good. You're gonna love it."

"Dad . . . I'm gonna help pay for college."

"No, you're not."

"Why not? I want to."

"I appreciate that, Sean, but . . ."

"Hey, you didn't call me Seany."

"I didn't? I guess you sounded like a grown-up just then, offering to help pay for college."

"I actually can, because . . ."

"No, Seany. You don't have to. There's something you don't know about. There's a little college fund put aside for you. I think it'll be enough."

"Really?"

"Yeah."

"Did Grandpa . . . ?"

"No. No. No. It's not money he stole, I swear to you. It's money Grandma had before she met Grandpa. My mother, besides being one of the most annoying people on the planet, turns out to be the real financial genius in the family. She's putting you and Jakey and Rachael through college."

We pulled into our driveway and went into the

house. I found out a lot of stuff on that pizza run. If you ever want to have a good talk with one of your parents, get them alone in the front seat.

"Okay, Seany. You're the boss. Where do we eat?"

"TV trays. I changed my mind."

chapter 46

It's been a couple of months since the night Stefanie told Dan Welch that if I want to write my own movie, they won't buy it.

Maybe you would have taken the $10,000 (or $50,000 if they actually made the movie). I just couldn't. I can't let *A Week with Your Grandparents* turn into something I might hate. I'm going to be in show business my whole life. My first big project has to be great. Or at least good.

Maybe Stefanie and her company knew what they were doing, but the more I work on the screenplay, the more I like it, and the more I think they made a big mistake.

I guess there's a good reason they were only my trial run company.

Since I didn't need my parents to sign that contract for me, I still haven't told them about any of this. I'm sure I will someday. What would be really cool is we go to the movies, we see *A Week with Your Grandparents*, it's really good, and at the end of the movie, right after *Directed by Whoever-it-is*, we see *Written by Sean Rosen*. I'm going to have to remember to put the credits at the end.

School is actually a little better these days. I really like Spanish. It makes more sense than French, at least the way you pronounce it. I guess whoever made up Spanish actually wanted people to know what they were saying. I practice with Javier's family. Now when I go over for dessert, they speak English and I speak Spanish. *"¿Un poco más dulce de leche, por favor?"*

Between school and writing the screenplay, I don't have as much time as I used to, so it's a good thing Ethan started helping me with the podcasts. It's fun. I keep asking him if he wants to do some of the interviews, but so far he doesn't.

Buzz's bannd played a concert at our school. They only have two songs so far, so it was a short concert. They're actually good. Ever since then, Brianna texts me about fifty times a day asking questions about Buzz. Uh-oh.

After the concert, Doug came over to me. I told him I liked the band. He asked me (nicely, for him) if I thought Dave Motts would like it. I told him to send me an MP3, and I'll send it to Dave.

I actually *will* send it to Dave Motts. I just got him an e-mail address. I don't want to bother Dan Welch. He's too busy with his main client.

To: Hank Hollywood (not his real name, President of my first-choice entertainment company)
From: Dan Welch Management

Dear Hank,

I represent Sean Rosen. He recently turned down an offer from Stefanie V. President at _____ (the name of her studio) to buy his movie *A Week with Your Grandparents*. Sean is currently writing the screenplay.

You may be familiar with Sean's podcasts, which he writes and produces. Some of them are available online. He's accomplished a lot for a thirteen-year-old.

Sean asked me to contact you because he has a very interesting idea. It's not an idea for a movie or a TV show. It's a whole new way of making and selling movies and TV shows, as well as games and theater. As Sean puts it, "I think it will change the way people think about entertainment."

I know that's hard to picture, but it was also hard to picture a major Hollywood studio wanting to buy a movie idea from a kid they never heard of before.

Sean has a lot of respect for your company, and you're his first choice for working together on his big idea. If you're interested, please let me know, and I'll be glad to set up a meeting for you and Sean on Skype.

Best,
Dan

acknowledgments

I couldn't have done this without my team of experts: Aurora, Chiara, Jeremy, Jordana, Jeremy, Savannah, Melinda, Simon, and a bunch of great kids at Ardsley Middle School. Thanks to my many grown-up friends and family who helped make this happen. Special thanks to Lisa Baron, Margie Gordon, Edgar McIntosh, Cameron Brindise, Bob Lipsyte, Bennett Ashley, Michael Steger, Tim Smith, Paul Zakris, and Kerry McCluggage, and continuous thanks to Gary Carlisle, Julie Just, and Virginia Duncan.

From the screenplay of

A Week With Your Grandparents
by Sean Rosen

Just to remind you:

Day 1: Chloe hurts Grandpa's feelings at dinner, apologizes, and the kids find out about the virtual reality time machine.

Day 2: The kids go back in time. Chloe meets Grandpa when he was 17. Chris meets Grandma when she was his age. He likes her in a way you usually don't like your grandmother, but then, not now.

Jeff Baron

DAY 3

At the kitchen table. Grandpa and
Chris eat cereal, and Chloe eats a
tiny box of raisins.

GRANDPA: (to Chloe): That's all
          you're eating?

CHLOE: That's all I'm eating right
          now. I'll have a Balance
          bar in about an hour.

CHRIS   She thinks it helps her on
          the balance beam.

CHLOE: He's hilarious.

CHRIS: Grandpa . . . can we go to
          the past again?

CHLOE: Yes. We can. We have to.

GRANDPA: (to Chris) Where would you
          go next time?

CHRIS: Oh, I don't know. Maybe
          the same place. You know,
          Grandma's school. I wasn't
          there very long.

CHLOE: We have to keep Grandma

※ 340 ※

away from the stop button.

CHRIS: What happened when she
           tried the machine?

GRANDPA: She won't tell me. And she
           won't get back in.

Grandma walks in.

GRANDMA: Well . . . I might go to
           someone else's past.

CHLOE: Whose?

GRANDMA: Roscoe's.

CHRIS: Your neighbor's dog?!

GRANDMA: I have a theory.

GRANDPA: Not this again.

CHLOE: What's your theory?

GRANDMA: Roscoe used to be a very
           sweet dog.

CUT TO: Roscoe standing on the grass
between the two houses, wagging his
tail. He's on a long leash attached to
his house.

GRANDPA: He wasn't so sweet.

GRANDMA: He actually was. Until we
          got the Toyota.

CUT TO: Roscoe barking like crazy and
yanking on his leash as Grandma and
Grandpa pull into their driveway in
their Toyota.

GRANDPA: A dog's personality doesn't
          change overnight.

GRANDMA: Unless he's been scared to
          death. (to Chris and Chloe)
          You may have noticed that
          your grandfather is not the
          world's best driver.

CHRIS: It's kind of like Space
          Mountain.

CHLOE: But with the lights on.

CHRIS: I usually keep my eyes
          closed.

GRANDPA: Okay, okay.

GRANDMA: Well maybe, just maybe,

> Grandpa missed the driveway
> the day he brought the car
> home, and almost hit Roscoe.
> I wasn't there.

GRANDPA: I didn't miss the driveway.

CHLOE: Yesterday, you did. Do dogs
have DNA?

CUT TO: Grandma, Chris, and Chloe
walking up to the next door neighbor's
front door. Grandma rings the doorbell.
We hear Roscoe barking. The door opens.

MRS. IRZYK: Well, hello.

GRANDMA: Hi, Beth. You've met
our grandchildren.

MRS. IRZYK: Hi. Did you want to
take your car out?
I'll make sure the dog
stays inside.

GRANDMA: No. Chris and Chloe
brought something for
Roscoe.

Chris holds up a doggie treat.

MRS. IRZYK: Oh, nice. (calls out)
               Roscoe!

Roscoe runs in, grabs the treat from
Chris's hand, then runs out.

MRS. IRZYK: He learned his manners
               from my husband.
CHLOE: Do you think Roscoe
               can be part of my
               science project?
MRS. IRZYK: You can't dissect him.

Chloe takes a glass slide from the
plastic container Grandma is holding.

CHLOE: I'm comparing human
               saliva with dog
               saliva.
MRS. IRZYK: Oh, sure. Roscoe will
               lick anything. Let me

hold the slide so he
doesn't eat it. (calls out)
Roscoe!

In slow motion, Roscoe runs in, and
then we see a close up of a big dog's
tongue licking the slide.

CUT TO: Grandpa's workroom. Grandma
is inside the time machine. Chris and
Chloe watch. Grandpa pushes TALK.

GRANDPA: Are you sure about this?

Then he pushes LISTEN.

GRANDMA: Roscoe, here I come.

. . .

What happens next?

Turn the page for a sneak peek at
Sean Rosen Is Not for Sale!

It's good. And it's funny. Trust me.
I should know,
because I represent Sean Rosen.

chapter 1

I'm late.

Buzz wanted to check out a new keyboard at the music store, and I wanted a donut, so we decided to meet in fifteen minutes. That was twenty minutes ago.

I had my donut (Boston cream—so good) and got one for Buzz, but then I had five minutes left, which felt like long enough to look around the used bookstore.

Unfortunately, the lady there recognized me.

"Hey, you're the boy who was looking for a book about movies."

"About *making* movies."

"Right. Make any movies yet?"

I *haven't* made any movies yet. But one of the big Hollywood studios *did* want to buy my movie idea. Seriously. They sent me a contract. 10,000 dollars right away, and 40,000 more if the movie got made.

You might think I'm crazy, but I said no. Which means now I have to try not to think about what I would do if I had the money. The new phone I would have, the new computer, the iPad. See? It's not easy. But I think I made the right decision.

For the next five minutes, the used-book lady told me a lot of things about growing zucchini. She's one of those people who doesn't stop between sentences. You never get a chance to say, "I have to go."

Finally someone came into the store and I could leave. I texted Buzz that I was on my way. I hate to be late.

ME:	Here's your donut. Sorry I'm late.
BUZZ:	You're not late.
ME:	Yes I am.

BUZZ:	No. You're not late until five minutes after the time.
ME:	I never heard of that. Are you sure?
BUZZ:	You didn't have to text me. I saw you coming.
ME:	How could you see me? I was two blocks away.
BUZZ:	No one else walks like that.
ME:	Like what? I was hurrying.
BUZZ:	You're always hurrying.
ME:	No I'm not.
BUZZ:	Right. Sometimes you stop and just stand there.
ME:	Because I'm thinking. Why? Do you always walk the same speed?

The next day after school, Ethan and I were standing outside on the steps. Well, on different steps. Ethan is about two feet taller than me, and it's a lot easier to talk this way.

"Do I walk funny?"

He thought about it for a second.

"Yeah."

"I *do*?"

"Yeah. So do I. So does everyone. Look."

He's right. Everyone has a funny walk. Everyone's arms look funny when they swing. That kid walks like he's in a race, possibly a race to the bathroom. That girl is walking and texting. She's approaching a tree. Look up! Look up! Ow.

She's okay. She's picking up her phone. She's walking. She's finishing her text.

"Thanks, Ethan."

Good. I'm too busy to worry about how I look when I walk. I have to get home and work on my screenplay for *A Week with Your Grandparents*. That's the movie I decided not to sell to Hollywood.

It's about this brother and sister, Chris and Chloe. He's fifteen and she's twelve. Their parents go away and they're stuck staying with you-know-who. Then they find out that Grandpa invented a virtual reality time machine that lets you spend time with someone on any day in their past. It's so cool. Chris and Chloe meet their grandparents when they were teenagers. The movie is sometimes funny and sometimes scary. The reason I didn't sell it was because I found out they wouldn't let me write it. It had to be an experienced screenwriter. Even though it was my idea.

I like most movies, but every once in a while, I hate one. I looked up some movies I hated, and guess what. They were all written by experienced screenwriters. I like this idea too much to let it be a movie I might hate.

I got home, and the painters were getting ready to leave. They've been painting the inside of our house. My parents are both at work, so the painter gave me our key.

"Here you go. All done. We left all the windows open in the family room. Stay out of there for a couple of hours. It'll be dry by then."

"Okay."

I stood in the kitchen and looked at the family room. They painted it last because we couldn't decide on a color. My dad wanted Club Room. You have no idea what color that is, right? How could you? It's dark green. I didn't like it. Neither did my mom.

She wanted Blush. She kept telling my dad and me, "It isn't pink. It's more of a . . . peach." First of all, I wouldn't call peach "not pink." Second, I don't want a pink family room. Neither does my dad.

I wanted it to be blue. I showed them seventeen blues that I liked. Any one of them would have been fine. But my mom and dad aren't "whatever Sean wants" kind of parents. I get one vote, just like everyone else. Blue got a total of one vote.

"Club Room wins. It's a combination of your two colors."

"Sorry, Dad. Green is not a combination of blue and pink."

"Blush *isn't* pink."

We ended up with Biscuit. It's light tan. I'm looking at it right now. It looks good. Thank goodness.

I dropped off my books upstairs. I thought about doing my homework, but I really want to see what happens next in my screenplay. That's what writing it feels like. Like I'm at the movies seeing it, then I just write down what I see. I don't know how it works, but I'm glad it does.

The place I like to work on my screenplay is the family room. Especially when no one else is there. When I write down what the people in the movie are saying, I actually say it out loud. If someone else is in the room, they think I'm talking to them, and they answer. It's distracting.

My parents don't know about this screenplay. They know I'm sort of creative. They know about my podcasts. They're the ones who pay for my subscription to *The Hollywood Reporter*. But they don't know I already started my career in show business. I thought about asking them whether I should sell my movie idea, but I didn't. They don't know the business. My dad is a plumber and my mom is a nurse. Dan Welch thinks I can write the screenplay. He's my manager.

I brought my laptop downstairs and took another look at the family room. I saw that I could definitely make it to the sofa without touching any walls. I *did* make it. I sat on the sofa and wrote for about a half hour.

I don't know why, but writing always makes me hungry. I got up and went to the kitchen to get a snack. I was still thinking about the screenplay, and I suddenly knew what happens next.

I turned to go back to my laptop to write it down, and a rug was where it usually isn't. I slipped and grabbed the wall so I wouldn't fall. He was right. The paint is still wet.

Now right in the middle of our beautiful new wall painted Biscuit is a perfect outline of my hand. If this was a TV detective show, it would be over in twenty seconds.

I wonder if I can fix it. I went to the garage, and I found a can of Biscuit the painters left. Maybe I can put my hand in the paint, then press it on the handprint on the wall.

Maybe not.

My parents still have a paper address book. I looked under P and found the painter's number. I called him and told him what happened. I said I would pay him if he could come over and fix it before my parents got home. He said okay. I hope

I have enough money.

He got here, looked at the wall, and got to work. I kept thinking of different ways to say "I'm sorry," but they all sounded stupid, so I didn't say anything. Also, I don't want to interrupt him. He probably gets paid by the hour.

It took him about twenty minutes. It looks perfect. I finally got the courage to say, "How much?"

"Are you going to listen next time when I tell you to stay out of the room?"

"Yes." I actually think I will.

"Okay. Yesterday you offered me lemonade without anyone telling you to. We're even."

My parents got home, and they both like the color of the family room. I didn't tell them about my little accident, but I also didn't try to stand in front of the place on the wall where my hand landed. We decided to go out for supper, because my mom said, "Anything we eat here is going to taste like paint. Not Biscuits."

I heard that I got a text during dinner, but we have a "no devices at the table" rule in our family, so I waited until we got back into the car to look.

Dug wants 2 no wot dave mots sez

It's Buzz. And it's not just texting language. Buzz can't spell. He's telling me that Doug (not Dug), who plays drums in Buzz's band, wants to know what Dave Motts (not Mots) thinks about the band's MP3.

If I heard anything from Dave Motts, I would have told them. Buzz knows that. I'm sure Doug made him send that text.

Doug and I used to be friends, but then he did something really mean to me, and a year later, I did something really mean to him. Then we didn't really talk anymore. Well, *I* didn't talk. He kept saying nasty things to me, which was actually a little scary. Doug was always one of the biggest kids, and last year he suddenly got a lot bigger.

But lately Doug has been acting a lot nicer to me. He thinks I can help the band. The band, for some strange reason, is called Taxadurmee. I asked Buzz about it.

ME: Why did you pick that name?
           It's creepy.
BUZZ: No it's not. It's cool.
ME: Do you know what it means?
BUZZ: No. No one does.
ME: *I* do. It means stuffing dead

animals so you can put them
on your wall.

BUZZ: No it doesn't.

ME: Look it up.

BUZZ: *You* look it up.

Anyway, Taxadurmee recorded two songs (that's all they have so far), and they sent me the MP3 to give to Dave Motts. They're hoping he'll like the songs, want to be their manager, get them a record contract, and make them rich and famous.

Dave Motts isn't a real person. Well, there may be a real person named Dave Motts, but the Dave Motts that Taxadurmee is waiting to hear from doesn't exactly exist. It's a long story.

It started when I tried to tell Buzz about the big movie studio wanting to buy my movie. That was a disaster. First, Buzz never heard of the studio, which is impossible. If you ever watched TV or ever went to the movies, you've heard of this studio. Seriously, *everyone* knows them.

I also told him about my manager, Dan Welch. I even said, "Welch, like the grape juice." Then, even though I told Buzz not to tell anyone about the movie or Dan Welch, he told Doug, except he said my manager's name is Dave (not Dan) Motts (like the *apple* juice). Anyway, now Buzz and Doug want "Dave Motts" to listen to their songs, so maybe he'll want to manage them too.

You're probably thinking Buzz is kind of dumb. He actually isn't. He just doesn't really pay attention. It's like his songs are playing in his head all the time, so he can't really hear anything else, including my manager's name.

Dan Welch . . . Dave Motts. It doesn't actually matter. Neither one of them is going to listen to that MP3. They can't. Neither of them is a real person.

I *had* to make up Dan Welch. The big companies in Hollywood won't even talk to you unless you have an agent or a manager. I learned this the hard way. I wrote a letter to one of the big studios, and their legal department sent me a six-page letter telling me to stay away from them until I have an agent or a manager.

I tried to get an agent. I tried to get a manager.

I couldn't. No one wanted to represent me. Then I thought up Dan Welch. His name came from our refrigerator. Dan from Dannon yogurt and Welch from Welch's grape juice.

I got him an email address, and when Dan Welch wrote to that same gigantic Hollywood studio that wouldn't talk to me, suddenly they wanted to talk to me. Soon they wanted to buy my movie idea. He turned out to be a very good manager.

I know it's me who actually writes Dan Welch's emails and chats, but even to me he feels like a separate person. I don't know what he looks like, but I know he's a little older than my parents, and he has kids.

He and I are so completely different. He never acts like a thirteen-year-old. Unfortunately, I usually do. His feelings don't get hurt as easily as mine. And he can say nice things about me that I would never say about myself.